A NICE, WELL-BRED GIRL

She brought a small automatic up from her side.

I looked at it. "Oh guns," I said. "Don't scare me with guns. I've lived with them all my life. I teethed on an old Derringer, single-shot, the kind the riverboat gamblers used to carry. As I got older I graduated to a lightweight sporting rifle, then a .303 target rifle and so on. I once made a bull at nine hundred yards with open sights. In case you don't know, the whole target looks the size of a postage stamp at nine hundred yards."

"A fascinating career," she said.

"Guns never settle anything," I said. "They are just a fast curtain to a bad second act."

She smiled faintly and transferred the gun to her left hand. With her right she grabbed the edge of her blouse at the collar line and with a quick decisive motion tore it to the waist.

By Raymond Chandler
Published by Ballantine Books:

KILLER IN THE RAIN

PLAYBACK

THE LONG GOODBYE

THE SIMPLE ART OF MURDER

PICKUP ON NOON STREET

TROUBLE IS MY BUSINESS

RAYMOND CHANDLER
PLAYBACK

BALLANTINE BOOKS • NEW YORK

Library of Congress Catalog Card Number: 58-9057

ISBN 0-345-32226-6

This edition published by arrangement with Houghton Mifflin
Company

Printed in Canada

First Ballantine Books Edition: January 1977
Sixth Printing: August 1984

To Jean and Helga

1

THE VOICE on the telephone seemed to be sharp and peremptory, but I didn't hear too well what it said—partly because I was only half awake and partly because I was holding the receiver upside down. I fumbled it around and grunted.

"Did you hear me? I said I was Clyde Umney, the lawyer."

"Clyde Umney, the lawyer. I thought we had several of them."

"You're Marlowe, aren't you?"

"Yeah. I guess so." I looked at my wrist watch. It was 6:30 A.M., not my best hour.

"Don't get fresh with me, young man."

"Sorry, Mr. Umney. But I'm not a young man. I'm old, tired and full of no coffee. What can I do for you, sir?"

"I want you to meet the Super Chief at eight o'clock, identify a girl among the passengers, follow her until she checks in somewhere, and then report to me. Is that clear?"

"No."

"Why not?" he snapped.

"I don't know enough to be sure I could accept the case."

"I'm Clyde Um—"

"Don't," I interrupted. "I might get hysterical. Just tell me the basic facts. Perhaps another investigator would suit you better. I never was an FBI man."

"Oh. My secretary, Miss Vermilyea, will be at your office in half an hour. She will have the necessary information for you. She is very efficient. I hope you are."

"I'm more efficient when I've had breakfast. Have her come here, would you?"

"Where is here?"

I gave him the address of my place on Yucca Avenue, and told him how she would find it.

"Very well," he said grudgingly, "but I want one thing very clear. The girl is not to know she is being followed. This is very important. I am acting for a very influential firm of Washington attorneys. Miss Vermilyea will advance you some expense money and pay you a retainer of two hundred and fifty dollars. I expect a high degree of efficiency. And let's not waste time talking."

"I'll do the best I can, Mr. Umney."

He hung up. I struggled out of bed, showered, shaved and was nuzzling my third cup of coffee when the door bell rang.

"I'm Miss Vermilyea, Mr. Umney's secretary," she said in a rather chintzy voice.

"Please come in."

She was quite a doll. She wore a white belted raincoat, no hat, a well-cherished head of platinum hair, booties to match the raincoat, a folding plastic umbrella, a pair of blue-gray eyes that looked at me as if I had said a dirty word. I helped her off with her raincoat. She smelled very nice. She had a pair of legs—so far as I could determine—that were not painful to look at. She wore night sheer stockings. I stared at them rather intently, especially when she crossed her legs and held out a cigarette to be lighted.

"Christian Dior," she said, reading my rather open mind. "I never wear anything else. A light, please."

"You're wearing a lot more today," I said, snapping a lighter for her.

"I don't greatly care for passes this early in the morning."

"What time would suit you, Miss Vermilyea?"

She smiled rather acidly, inventoried her handbag and tossed me a manila envelope. "I think you'll find everything you need in this."

"Well—not quite everything."

"Get on with it, you goof. I've heard all about you. Why do you think Mr. Umney chose you? He didn't. I did. And stop looking at my legs."

I opened the envelope. It contained another sealed envelope and two checks made out to me. One, for $250, was marked "Retainer, as an advance against fees for professional services." The other was for $200 and was marked "Advance to Philip Marlowe for necessary expenses."

"You will account for the expenses to me, in exact detail," Miss Vermilyea said. "And buy your own drinks."

The other envelope I didn't open—not yet. "What makes Umney think I'll take a case I know nothing about?"

"You'll take it. You're not asked to do anything wrong. You have my word for that."

"What else do I have?"

"Oh, we might discuss that over a drink some rainy evening, when I'm not too busy."

"You've sold me."

I opened the other envelope. It contained a photograph of a girl. The pose suggested a natural ease, or a lot of experience in being photographed. It showed darkish hair which might possibly have been red, a wide clear forehead, serious eyes, high cheekbones, nervous nostrils and a mouth which was not giving anything away. It was a fine-drawn, almost a taut face, and not a happy one.

"Turn it over," Miss Vermilyea said.

On the back there was clearly typed material.

"Name: Eleanor King. Height five feet four inches. Age about 29. Hair dark reddish brown, thick, with a natural wave. Erect carriage, low distinct voice, well dressed but not overdressed. Conservative make-up. No visible scars. Characteristic mannerisms: habit of moving her eyes without moving her head when entering a room. Scratches palm of right hand when tense. Left-handed but adept in concealing it. Plays fast tennis, swims and dives beautifully, holds her liquor. No convictions, but prints on file."

"Been in the coop," I said, looking up at Miss Vermilyea.

"I have no information beyond what is there. Just follow your instructions."

"No name, Miss Vermilyea. At twenty-nine a dish like this would almost certainly have been married. There's no mention of a wedding ring or any other jewels. That makes me wonder."

She glanced at her watch. "Better do your wondering at the Union Station. You haven't much time." She stood up. I helped her on with her white raincoat and opened the door.

"You came in your own car?"

"Yes." She went halfway out and turned. "There's one thing I like about you. You don't paw. And you have nice manners—in a way."

"It's a rotten technique—to paw."

"And there's one thing I don't like about you. Guess what it is."

"Sorry. No idea—except that some people hate me for being alive."

"I didn't mean that."

I followed her down the steps and opened her car door for her. It was a cheap job, a Fleetwood Cadillac. She nodded briefly and slid down the hill.

I went back up and loaded a few things into an overnight bag, just in case.

2

THERE WAS nothing to it. The Super Chief was on time, as it almost always is, and the subject was as easy to spot as a kangaroo in a dinner jacket. She wasn't carrying anything but a paperback which she dumped in the first trash can she came to. She sat down and looked at the floor. An unhappy girl, if ever I saw one. After a while she got up and went to the book rack. She left it without picking anything out, glanced at the big clock on the wall and shut herself in a telephone booth. She talked to someone after putting a handful of silver into the slot. Her expression didn't change at all. She hung up and went to the magazine rack, picked up a *New Yorker*, looked at her watch again, and sat down to read.

She was wearing a midnight blue tailor-made suit with a white blouse showing at the neck and a big sapphire blue lapel pin which would probably have matched her earrings, if I could see her ears. Her hair was a dusky red. She looked like her photograph, but a little taller than I expected. Her dark blue ribbon hat had a short veil hanging from it. She was wearing gloves.

After a while she moved across the arches outside of which the taxis wait. She looked left at the coffee shop, turned and went into the main waiting room, glanced at the drugstore and newsstand, the information booth, and the people sitting on the clean wooden benches. Some of the ticket windows were open, some not. She wasn't interested in them. She sat down again and looked up at the big clock. She pulled off her right glove and set her wrist watch, a small plain platinum toy without jewels. Mentally I put Miss Vermilyea beside her. She didn't look soft or prissy or prudish, but she made the Vermilyea look like a pick-up.

She didn't stay long sitting down this time, either. She got up and strolled. She went out into the patio and came back and went into the drugstore and stayed some time at the paper-book rack. Two things were obvious. If anyone was going to meet her, the date hadn't been for train time. She looked like a girl waiting between trains. She went into the coffee shop. She sat down at one of the plastic top tables, read the menu, and then started to read her magazine. A waitress came with the inevitable glass of ice water, and the menu. The subject gave an order. The waitress went away, the subject went on reading her magazine. It was about nine-fifteen.

I went out through the arches to where a redcap was waiting by the taxi starter. "You work the Super Chief?" I asked him.

"Yeah. Part of it." He glanced without too deep interest at the buck I was teasing with my fingers.

"I was expecting someone on the Washington-San Diego through car. Anybody get off?"

"You mean get off permanent, baggage and all?"

I nodded.

He thought about it, studying me with intelligent chestnut eyes. "One passenger get off," he said at last. "What your friend look like?"

I described a man. Someone who looked something like Edward Arnold. The redcap shook his head.

"Can't help you, mister. What got off don't look like that at all. Your friend probably still on the train. They don't have to get off the through car. She gets hitched on to Seventy-Four. Leaves here eleven-thirty. The train ain't made up yet."

"Thanks," I said, and gave him the dollar. The subject's baggage was still on the train, which was all I wanted to know.

I went back to the coffee shop and looked in through the glass wall.

Subject was reading her magazine and toying with coffee and a snail. I moved over to a phone booth and called a garage I knew well and asked them to send somebody for my car if I didn't call again by noon. They'd done this often enough to have a spare key on hand. I went out to the car and got my overnight bag out of it and into a two-bit locker. In the enormous waiting room, I bought a round trip to San Diego and trotted back to the coffee shop once again.

Subject was in place, but no longer alone. A guy was across the table from her smiling and talking, and one look was enough to show that she knew him and regretted it. He was California from the tips of his port wine loafers to the buttoned and tieless brown and yellow checked shirt inside his rough cream sports jacket. He was about six feet one, slender, with a thin conceited face and too many teeth. He was twisting a piece of paper in his hand.

The yellow handkerchief in his outside breast pocket sprayed out like a small bunch of daffodils. And one thing was as clear as distilled water. The girl didn't want him there.

He went on talking and twitching the paper. Finally he shrugged and got up from his chair. He reached over and ran a fingertip down her cheek. She jerked back. Then he opened the twisted paper and laid it carefully down in front of her. He waited, smiling.

Her eyes went down to it very, very slowly. Her eyes held on it. Her hand moved to take it, but his was quicker. He put it away in his pocket, still smiling. Then he took out one of those pocket notebooks with perforated pages, and wrote something with a clip pen and tore the sheet out and put that down in front of

her. That she could have. She took it, read it, put it in
her purse. At last she looked at him. And at last she
smiled at him. My guess was that it took quite an effort. He reached across to pat her hand, then walked
away from the table and out.

He shut himself in a phone booth, dialed, and talked
for quite a while. He came out, found himself a redcap
and went with the redcap to a locker. Out came a light
oyster-white suitcase and a matching overnight case.
The redcap carried them through the doors to the
parking lot and followed him to a sleek two-toned
Buick Roadmaster, the solid top convertible type that
isn't convertible. The redcap put the stuff in behind the
tipped seat, took his money, went away. The guy in the
sports coat and yellow handkerchief got in and backed
his car out and then stopped long enough to put on
dark glasses and light a cigarette. After that he was
gone. I wrote down the license number and went back
into the station.

The next hour was three hours long. The girl left the
coffee shop and read her magazine in the waiting room.
Her mind wasn't on it. She kept turning back to see
what she had read. Part of the time she didn't read at
all, just held the magazine and looked at nothing. I had
an early morning edition of the evening paper and behind it I watched her and added up what I had in my
head. None of it was solid fact. It just helped to pass the
time.

The guy who had sat at the table with her had come
off the train, since he had baggage. It could have been
her train and he could have been the passenger that
got off her car. Her attitude made it pretty clear that
she didn't want him around, and his that that was too
bad but if she would glance at his piece of paper she
would change her mind. And apparently she did. Since
this happened after they got off the train when it could
have happened more quietly before, then it followed
that he didn't have his piece of paper on the train.

At this point the girl got up abruptly and went to the
newsstand and came back with a pack of cigarettes.

She tore it open and lit one. She smoked awkwardly as if she wasn't used to it, and while she smoked her attitude seemed to change, to become more flashy and hard, as if she was deliberately vulgarizing herself for some purpose. I looked at the wall clock: 10.47. I went on with my thinking.

The twist of paper had looked like a newspaper clipping. She had tried to grab it, he hadn't let her. Then he had written some words on a piece of blank paper and given them to her and she had looked at him and smiled. Conclusion: the dreamboat had something on her and she had to pretend to like it.

Next point was that earlier on he had left the station and gone somewhere, perhaps to get his car, perhaps to get the clipping, perhaps anything you like. That meant he wasn't afraid that she would run out on him, and that reinforced the idea that he hadn't at that time disclosed everything he was holding up his sleeve but had disclosed some of it. Could be he wasn't sure himself. Had to check. But now having shown her his hole card he had gone off in a Buick with his baggage. Therefore he was no longer afraid of losing her. Whatever held them together was strong enough to keep on holding them.

At 11.05 I tossed all this out of the window and started with a fresh premise. I got nowhere. At 11:10 the public address system said Number Seventy-Four on Track Eleven was now ready to receive passengers for Santa Ana, Oceanside, Del Mar and San Diego. A bunch of people left the waiting room, including the girl. Another bunch was already going through the gate. I watched her through and went back to the phone booths. I dropped my dime and dialed the number of Clyde Umney's office.

Miss Vermilyea answered by giving the phone number only.

"This is Marlowe. Mr. Umney in?"

Her voice was formal saying: "I'm sorry, Mr. Umney is in court. May I take a message?"

"Am in contact and leaving by train for San Diego, or some intermediate stop. Can't tell which yet."

"Thank you. Anything else?"

"Yeah, the sun's shining and our friend is no more on the lam than you are. She ate breakfast in the coffee shop which has a glass wall towards the concourse. She sat in the waiting room with a hundred and fifty other people. And she could have stayed on the train out of sight."

"I have all that, thank you. I'll get it to Mr. Umney as soon as possible. You have no firm opinion then?"

"I have one firm opinion. That you're holding out on me."

Her voice changed abruptly. Somebody must have left the office. "Listen, chum, you were hired to do a job. Better do it and do it right. Clyde Umney draws a lot of water in this town."

"Who wants water, beautiful? I take mine straight with a beer chaser. I might make sweeter music if I was encouraged."

"You'll get paid, shamus—if you do a job. Not otherwise. Is that clear?"

"That's the nicest thing you ever said to me, sweetheart. Goodbye now."

"Listen, Marlowe," she said with sudden urgency. "I didn't mean to be rough with you. This is very important to Clyde Umney. If he doesn't come through, he might lose a very valuable connection. I was just sounding off."

"I liked it, Vermilyea. It did things to my subconscious. I'll call in when I can."

I hung up, went through the gate, down the ramp, walked about from here to Ventura to get to Track Eleven and climbed aboard a coach that was already full of the drifting cigarette smoke that is so kind to your throat and nearly always leaves you with one good lung. I filled and lit a pipe and added to the general frowst.

The train pulled out, dawdled interminably through the yards and the back stretches of East L.A., picked

up a little speed and made its first stop at Santa Ana.
Subject did not get off. At Oceanside and Del Mar the
same. At San Diego I hopped off quickly, chartered a
cab, and then waited eight minutes outside the old
Spanish station for the redcaps to come out with the
baggage. Then the girl came out too.

She didn't take a cab. She crossed the street and
rounded the corner to a U-Drive outfit and after a longish interval came out again looking disappointed. No
driver's license, no U-Drive. You'd think she would
have known that.

She took a cab this time and it did a U turn and
started north. Mine did the same. I had a little difficulty with my driver about the tail job.

"That's something you read about in books, mister.
We don't do it in Dago."

I passed him a fin and the 4 × 2½ photostat of my
license. He looked them over, both of them. He looked
off up the block.

"Okay, but I report it," he said. "The dispatcher
may report it to the Police Business Office. That's the
way it is here, chum."

"Sounds like the kind of city I ought to live in," I
said. "And you've lost the tail. He turned left two
blocks ahead."

The driver handed me back my wallet. "Lost my left
eye," he said tersely. "What you think a two-way radiophone is for?" He picked it up and talked into it.

He turned left at Ash Street to Highway 101 and we
merged with the traffic and kept going at a peaceable
forty. I stared at the back of his head.

"You don't have a worry in the world," the driver
told me over his shoulder. "This five is on top of the
fare, huh?"

"Right. And why don't I have a worry in the
world?"

"The passenger's going to Esmeralda. That's twelve
miles north of here on the ocean front. Destination,
unless changed en route—and if it is I'll get told—a

hotel joint called the Rancho Descansado. That's Spanish for relax, take it easy."

"Hell, I didn't need a cab at all," I said.

"You got to pay for the service, mister. We ain't buying groceries giving it away."

"You Mexican?"

"We don't call ourselves that, mister. We call ourselves Spanish-Americans. Born and raised in the USA. Some of us don't hardly speak Spanish any more."

"*Es gran lástima,*" I said. "*Una lengua muchísima hermosa.*"

He turned his head and grinned. "*Tiene Vd. razón, amigo. Estoy muy bien de acuerdo.*"

We went on to Torrance Beach, through there and swung out towards the point. From time to time the hackie talked into his radiophone. He turned his head enough to speak to me again.

"You want to keep out of sight?"

"What about the other driver? Will he tell his passenger she's being tailed?"

"He ain't been told hisself. That's why I asked you."

"Pass him and get there ahead, if you can. That's five more on the top."

"A cinch. He won't even see me. I can rib him later on over a bottle of Tecate."

We went through a small shopping center, then the road widened and the houses on one side looked expensive and not new, while the houses on the other side looked very new and still not cheap. The road narrowed again and we were in a 25 mile zone. My driver cut to the right, wound through some narrow streets, jumped a stop sign, and before I had had time to size up where we were going, we were sliding down into a canyon with the Pacific glinting off to the left beyond a wide shallow beach with two lifeguard stations on open metal towers. At the bottom of the canyon the driver started to turn in through the gates, but I stopped him. A large sign, gold script on a green background, said: *El Rancho Descansado.*

"Get out of sight," I said. "I want to make sure."

He swung back on the highway, drove fast down beyond the end of the stucco wall, then cut into a narrow
winding road on the far side and stopped. A gnarled
eucalyptus with a divided trunk hung over us. I got out
of the cab, put dark glasses on, strolled down to the
highway and leaned against a bright red jeep with the
name of a service station painted on it. A cab came
down the hill and turned into the Rancho Descansado.
Three minutes passed. The cab came out empty and
turned back up the hill. I went back to my driver.

"Cab No. 423," I said. "That check?"

"That's your pigeon. What now?"

"We wait. What's the layout over there?"

"Bungalows with car ports. Some single, some double. Office in a small one down front. Rates pretty
steep in season. This is slack time around here. Half
price probably and plenty of room."

"We wait five minutes. Then I check in, drop my
suitcase, and look for a car to rent."

He said that was easy. In Esmeralda there were
three places that rented cars, time and mileage, any
make you wanted.

We waited the five minutes. It was now just past
three o'clock. I was empty enough to steal the dog's
dinner.

I paid my driver off, watched him leave, and went
across the highway and into the office.

3

I LEANED a polite elbow on the counter and looked across at the happy-faced young guy in the polka-dotted bow tie. I looked from him to the girl at the small PBX against the side wall. She was an outdoorsy type with shiny make-up and a horse tail of medium blond hair sticking out at the back of her noodle. But she had nice large soft eyes and when they looked at the clerk they glistened. I looked back at him and choked back a snarl. The girl at the PBX swung her horse tail in an arc and put the eye on me also.

"I'd be glad to show you what we have vacant, Mr. Marlowe," the young guy said politely. "You can register later, if you decide to stay here. About how long would you be likely to want accommodations?"

"Only as long as she does," I said. "The girl in the blue suit. She just registered. Using what name I wouldn't know."

He and the PBX girl stared at me. Both their faces had the same expression of distrust mixed with curiosity. There are a hundred ways of playing this scene. But this was a new one for me. In no city hotel in the world would it work. It might work here. Mostly because I didn't give a damn.

"You don't like that, do you?" I said.

14

He shook his head slightly. "At least you're frank about it."

"I'm tired of being cagey. I'm worn out with it. Did you notice her ring finger?"

"Why no, I didn't." He looked at the PBX girl. She shook her head and kept her eyes on my face.

"No wedding ring," I said. "Not any more. All gone. All broken up. All the years—ah, the hell with it. I've followed her all the way from—well, never mind where. She won't even speak to me. What am I doing here? Making a damn fool of myself." I turned away quickly and blew my nose. I had their attention. "I'd better go somewhere else," I said, turning back.

"You want to make it up and she won't," the PBX girl said quietly.

"Yes."

"I'm sympathetic," the young guy said. "But you know how it is, Mr. Marlowe. A hotel has to be very careful. These situations can lead to anything—even shootings."

"Shootings?" I looked at him with wonder. "Good God, what sort of people do that?"

He leaned both arms on the desk. "Just what would you like to do, Mr. Marlowe?"

"I'd like to be near her—in case she needs me. I wouldn't speak to her. I wouldn't even knock at her door. But she would know I was there and she'd know why. I'd be waiting. I'll always be waiting."

The girl loved it now. I was up to my neck in the soft corn. I took a deep slow breath and shot for the grand prize. "And I don't somehow like the look of the guy who brought her here," I said.

"Nobody brought her here—except a cabdriver," the clerk said. But he knew what I meant all right.

The PBX girl half smiled. "He doesn't mean that, Jack. He means the reservation."

Jack said, "I kind of gathered as much, Lucille. I'm not so dumb." Suddenly he brought a card out from the desk and put it down in front of me. A registration card. Across the corner diagonally was written the name Larry Mitchell. In a very different writing in the proper places: (Miss) Betty Mayfield, West Chatham, New York. Then in the top left-hand corner in the same writing as Larry Mitchell a date, a time, a price, a number.

"You're very kind," I said. "So she's gone back to her maiden name. It's legal, of course."

"Any name is legal, if there's no intent to defraud. You would like to be next door to her?"

I widened my eyes. Maybe they glistened a little. Nobody ever tried harder to make them glisten.

"Look," I said, "it's damn nice of you. But you can't do it. I'm not going to make any trouble, but you can't be sure. It's your job if I pulled anything."

"Okay," he said. "I've got to learn some day. You look all right to me. Just don't tell anybody." He took the pen from its cup and held it out. I signed my name with an address on East Sixty-first Street, New York City.

Jack looked at it. "That's near Central Park, isn't it?" he asked idly.

"Three blocks and a bit," I said. "Between Lexington and Third Avenue."

He nodded. He knew where it was. I was in. He reached for a key.

"I'd like to leave my suitcase here," I said, "and go get something to eat and maybe rent a car, if I can. You could have it put in the room for me?"

Sure. He could do that for me easy. He took me outside and pointed up through a grove of saplings. The cottages were allover shingled, white with green roofs. They had porches with railings. He showed me mine through the trees. I thanked him. He started back in and I said, "Look, there's one thing. She may check out when she knows."

He smiled. "Of course. Nothing we can do about that, Mr. Marlowe. Lots of guests only stay a night or two—except in summer. We don't expect to be filled up this time of year."

He went on into the office cottage and I heard the girl say to him: "He's kind of cute, Jack—but you shouldn't have done it."

I heard his answer too. "I hate that guy Mitchell— even if he is a pal of the owner."

4

THE ROOM was bearable. It had the usual concrete couch, chairs without cushions, a small desk against the front wall, a walk-in closet with a built-in chest, a bathroom with a Hollywood bath and neon shaving lights beside the mirror over the basin, a small kitchen-ette with a refrigerator and a white stove, a three-bur-ner electric. In a wall cupboard over the sink enough dishes and stuff. I got some ice cubes and made myself a drink with the bottle from my suitcase, sipped it and sat in a chair listening, leaving the windows shut and the venetian blinds dark. I heard nothing next door, then I heard the toilet flush. Subject was in residence. I finished the drink, killed a cigarette and studied the wall heater on the party wall. It consisted of two long frosted bulbs in a metal box. It didn't look as if it would throw out much heat, but in the closet there was a plug-in fan heater with a thermostat and a three-way plug, which made it 220 volts. I slipped off the chro-mium grill guard of the wall heater and twisted out the frosted bulbs. I got a doctor's stethoscope out of my suitcase and held it against the metal backing and listened. If there was another similar heater back against it in the next room, and there almost certainly would be, all I had between the two rooms was a metal panel and some insulation, probably a bare minimum of that.

I heard nothing for a few minutes, then I heard a telephone being dialed. The reception was perfect. A woman's voice said: "Esmeralda 4-1499, please."

It was a cool contained voice, medium pitch, very little expression in it except that it sounded tired. It was the first time I had heard her voice in all the hours I had been following her.

There was a longish pause, then she said: "Mr. Larry Mitchell, please."

Another pause, but shorter. Then: "This is Betty Mayfield, at the Rancho Descansado." She pronounced the "a" in Descansado wrong. Then: "Betty Mayfield, I said. Please don't be stupid. Do you want me to spell it for you?"

The other end had things to say. She listened. After a while she said: "Apartment 12C. You ought to know. You made the reservation . . . Oh. I see . . . Well, all right. I'll be here."

She hung up. Silence. Complete silence. Then the voice in there said slowly and emptily: "Betty Mayfield, Betty Mayfield, Betty Mayfield. Poor Betty. You were a nice girl once—long ago."

I was sitting on the floor on one of the striped cushions with my back to the wall. I got up carefully, laid the stethoscope down on the cushion and went to lie on the day bed. After a while he would arrive. She was in there waiting for him, because she had to. She'd had to come there for the same reason. I wanted to know what it was.

He must have been wearing crepe soles because I didn't hear anything until the buzzer sounded next door. Also, he hadn't driven his car up to the cottage. I got down on the floor and went to work with the stethoscope.

She opened the door, he came in and I could imagine the smile on his face as he said: "Hello, Betty. Betty Mayfield is the name, I believe. I like it."

"It was my name originally." She closed the door.

He chuckled. "I suppose you were wise to change it. But how about the initials on your luggage?"

I didn't like his voice any better than his smile. It was high and cheerful, almost bubbly with sly good humor. There was not quite a sneer in it, but close enough. It made me clamp my teeth.

"I suppose," she said dryly, "that was the first thing you noticed."

"No, baby. *You* were the first thing I noticed. The mark of a wedding ring but no wedding ring was the second. The initials were only the third."

"Don't call me 'baby', you cheap blackmailer," she said with a sudden muted fury.

It didn't faze him in the least. "I may be a blackmailer, honey, but"——another conceited chuckle——"I'm certainly not cheap."

She walked, probably away from him. "Do you want a drink? I see you have a bottle with you."

"It might make me lascivious."

"There's only one thing about you I'm afraid of, Mr. Mitchell," the girl said coolly. "Your big loose mouth. You talk too much and you like yourself too well. We'd better understand each other. I like Esmeralda. I've been here before and I always wanted to come back. It's nothing but sheer bad luck that you live here and that you were on the train that was taking me here. It was the worst kind of luck that you should have recognized me. But that's all it is—bad luck."

"Good luck for me, honey," he drawled.

"Perhaps," she said, "if you don't put too much pressure on it. If you do, it's liable to blow up in your face."

There was a brief silence. I could see them in my imagination, staring at each other. His smile might be getting a little nervous, but not much.

"All I've got to do," he said quietly, "is pick up the phone and call the San Diego papers. You want publicity? I can arrange it for you."

"I came here to get rid of it," she said bitterly.

He laughed. "Sure, by an old coot of a judge falling to pieces with senile decay, and in the only state in the Union—and I've checked on that—where it could happen after the jury said otherwise. You've changed your name twice. If your story got printed out here—and it's a pretty good story, honey—I guess you'd have to change your name again—and start traveling a little more. Gets kind of tiresome, doesn't it?"

"That's why I'm here," she said. "That's why you're here. How much do you want? I realize it will only be a down payment."

"Have I said anything about money?"

"You will," she said. "And keep your voice down."

"The cottage is all yours, honey. I walked around it before I came in. Doors closed, windows shut, blinds drawn, car ports empty. I can check with the office, if you're nervous. I've got friends around here—people you need to know, people who can make life pleasant for you. Socially this is a tough town to break into. And it's a damn dull town if you're on the outside looking in."

"How did *you* get in, Mr. Mitchell?"

"My old man is a big shot in Toronto. We don't get on and he won't have me around home. But he's still my old man and he's still the real thing, even if he does pay me to stay away."

She didn't answer him. Her steps went away. I heard her in the kitchen making the usual sounds connected with getting ice out of a tray of cubes. The water ran, the steps came back.

"I'd like one myself," she said. "Perhaps I've been rude to you. I'm tired."

"Sure," he said equably. "You're tired." A pause. "Well, here's to when you're not tired. Say about seven-thirty this evening at The Glass Room. I'll pick you up. Nice place for dinner. Dancing. Quiet. Exclusive, if that means anything any more. Belongs to the Beach Club. They don't have a table unless they know you. I'm among friends there."

"Expensive?" she asked.

"A little. Oh yes—and that reminds me. Until my monthly check comes in, you could let me have a couple of dollars." He laughed. "I'm surprised at myself. I did mention money after all."

"A couple of dollars?"

"A couple of hundred would be better."

"Sixty dollars is all I have—until I can open an account or cash some traveler's checks."

"You can do that at the office, baby."

"So I can. Here's fifty. I don't want to spoil you, Mr. Mitchell."

"Call me Larry. Be human."

"Should I?" Her voice had changed. There was a hint of invitation in it. I could imagine the slow smile of pleasure on his face. Then I guess from the silence that he had grabbed her and she had let him. Finally her voice was a little muffled, saying: "That's enough, Larry. Be nice now and run along. I'll be ready at seven-thirty."

"One more for the road."

In a moment the door opened and he said something I didn't catch. I got up and went to the window and took a careful look through the slats of the blind. A floodlight was turned on in one of the tall trees. Under it I saw him stroll off up the slope and disappear. I went back to the heater panel and for a while I heard nothing and wasn't sure what I was listening for. But I knew soon enough.

There was quick movement back and forth, the sound of drawers being pulled open, the snap of a lock, the bump of a lifted lid against something.

She was packing up to leave.

I screwed the long frosted bulbs back into the heater and replaced the grille and put the stethoscope back in my suitcase. The evening was getting chilly. I slipped my jacket on and stood in the middle of the floor. It was getting dark and no light on. I just stood there and thought it over. I could go to the phone and make a report and by that time she could be on her way in another cab to another train or plane to another destination. She could go anywhere she liked, but there would always be a dick to meet the train if it meant enough to the big important people back in Washington. There would always be a Larry Mitchell or a reporter with a good memory. There would always be the little oddness to be noticed and there would always be somebody to notice it. You can't run away from yourself.

I was doing a cheap sneaky job for people I didn't like, but—that's what you hire out for, chum. They pay the bills, you dig the dirt. Only this time I could taste it. She didn't look like a tramp and she didn't look like a crook. Which meant only that she could be both with more success than if she had.

5

I OPENED the door and went along to the next and pushed the little buzzer. Nothing moved inside. There was no sound of steps. Then came the click of a chain set in the groove and the door opened a couple of inches on light and emptiness. The voice said from behind the door: "Who is it?"

"Could I borrow a cup of sugar?"

"I haven't any sugar."

"Well how about a couple of dollars until my check comes in?"

More silence. Then the door opened to the limit of the chain and her face edged into the opening and shadowed eyes stared out at me. They were just pools in the dark. The floodlight set high in the tree glinted on them obliquely.

"Who are you?"

"I'm your next door neighbor. I was having a nap and voices woke me. The voices spoke words. I was intrigued."

"Go somewhere else and be intrigued."

"I could do that, Mrs. King—pardon me, Miss Mayfield—but I'm not sure you'd want me to."

She didn't move and her eyes didn't waver. I shook a cigarette out of a pack and tried to push up the top of my Zippo with my thumb and rotate the wheel. You should be able to do it one-handed. You can too, but it's an awkward process. I made it at last and got the cigarette going, yawned, and blew smoke out through my nose.

"What do you do for an encore?" she asked.

"To be strictly kosher I should call L.A. and tell the party who sent me. Maybe I could be talked out of it."

"God," she said fervently, "two of them in one afternoon. How lucky can a girl get?"

"I don't know," I said. "I don't know anything. I think I've been played for a sucker, but I'm not sure."

"Wait a minute." She shut the door in my face. She wasn't gone long. The chain came out of the groove inside and the door came open.

I went in slowly and she stepped back and away from me. "How much did you hear? And shut the door, please."

I shut it with my shoulder and leaned against it.

"The tag end of a rather nasty conversation. The walls here are as thin as a hoofer's wallet."

"You in show business?"

"Just the opposite of show business. I'm in the hide-and-seek business. My name is Philip Marlowe. You've seen me before."

"Have I?" She walked away from me in little cautious steps and went over by her open suitcase. She leaned against the arm of a chair. "Where?"

"Union Station in L.A. We waited between trains, you and I. I was interested in you. I was interested in what went on between you and Mr. Mitchell—that's his name, isn't it? I didn't hear anything and I didn't see much because I was outside the coffee shop."

"So what interested you, you great big lovable something or other?"

"I've just told you part of it. The other thing that interested me was how you changed after your talk with him. I watched you work at it. It was very deliberate. You made yourself over into just another flip hardboiled modern cutie. Why?"

"What was I before?"

"A nice quiet well-bred girl."

"That was the act," she said. "The other was my natural personality. Which goes with something else." She brought a small automatic up from her side.

I looked at it. "Oh guns," I said. "Don't scare me with guns. I've lived with them all my life. I teethed on an old Derringer, single-shot, the kind the riverboat gamblers used to carry. As I got older I graduated to a lightweight sporting rifle, then a .303 target rifle and so on. I once made a bull at nine hundred yards with open sights. In case you don't know, the whole target looks the size of a postage stamp at nine hundred yards."

"A fascinating career," she said.

"Guns never settle anything," I said. "They are just a fast curtain to a bad second act."

She smiled faintly and transferred the gun to her left hand. With her right she grabbed the edge of her blouse at the collar line and with a quick decisive motion tore it to the waist.

"Next," she said, "but there's no hurry about it, I turn the gun in my hand like this"—she put it back in her right hand, but held it by the barrel—"I slam myself on the cheekbone with the butt. I do a beautiful bruise."

"And after that," I said, "you get the gun into its proper position and release the safety catch and pull the trigger, just about the time I get through the lead column in the Sports Section."

"You wouldn't get halfway across the room."

I crossed my legs and leaned back and lifted the green glass ash tray from the table beside the chair and balanced it on my knee and held the cigarette I was smoking between the first and second fingers of my right hand.

"I wouldn't get any of the way across the room. I'd be sitting here like this, quite comfortable and relaxed."

"But slightly dead," she said. "I'm a good shot and it isn't nine hundred yards."

"Then you try to sell the cops your account of how I tried to attack you and you defended yourself."

She tossed the gun into her suitcase and laughed. It sounded like a genuine laugh with real amusement in it. "Sorry," she said. "You sitting there with your legs crossed and a hole in your head and me trying to explain how I shot you to defend my honor—the picture makes me a little lightheaded."

She dropped into a chair and leaned forward with her chin cupped in a hand, the elbow propped on her knee, her face taut and drained, her dark red hair framing it too luxuriantly, so that her face looked smaller than it should have.

"Just what are you doing to me, Mr. Marlowe? Or is it the other way around—what I can do for you in return for you not doing anything at all?"

"Who is Eleanor King? What was she in Washington, D.C.? Why did she change her name somewhere along the way and have the initials taken off her bag? Odds and ends like that are what you could tell me. You probably won't."

"Oh, I don't know. The porter took the initials off my things. I told him I had had a very unhappy marriage and was divorced and had been given the right to resume my unmarried name. Which is Elizabeth or Betty Mayfield. That could all be true, couldn't it?"

"Yeah. But it doesn't explain Mitchell."

She leaned back and relaxed. Her eyes stayed watchful. "Just an acquaintance I made along the way. He was on the train."

I nodded. "But he came down here in his own car. He made the reservation here for you. He's not liked by the people here, but apparently he is a friend of someone with a lot of influence."

"An acquaintance on a train or a ship sometimes develops very quickly," she said.

"So it seems. He even touched you for a loan. Very fast work. And I got the impression you didn't care for him too well."

"Well," she said. "so what? But as a matter of fact

I'm crazy about him." She turned her hand over and looked down at it. "Who hired you, Mr. Marlowe, and for what?"

"A Los Angeles lawyer, acting on instructions from back east. I was to follow you and check you in somewhere. Which I did. But now you're getting ready to move out. I'm going to have to start over again."

"But with me knowing you're there," she said shrewdly. "So you'll have a much harder job of it. You're a private detective of some sort, I gather."

I said I was. I had killed my cigarette some time back. I put the ash tray back on the table and stood up.

"Harder for me, but there are lots of others, Miss Mayfield."

"Oh, I'm sure there are, and all such nice little men. Some of them are even fairly clean."

"The cops are not looking for you. They'd have had you easily. It was known about your train. I even got a photo of you and a description. But Mitchell can make you do just what he wants. Money isn't all he'll want."

I thought she flushed a little, but the light didn't strike her face directly. "Perhaps so," she said. "And perhaps I don't mind."

"You mind."

She stood up suddenly and came near me. "You're in a business that doesn't pay fortunes, aren't you?"

I nodded. We were very close now.

"Then what would it be worth to you to walk out of here and forget you ever saw me?"

"I'd walk out of here for free. As for the rest, I have to make a report."

"How much?" She said it as if she meant it. "I can afford a substantial retainer. That's what you call it, I've heard. A much nicer word than blackmail."

"It doesn't mean the same thing."

"It could. Believe me, it can mean just that—even with some lawyers and doctors. I happen to know."

"Tough break, huh?"

"Far from it, shamus. I'm the luckiest girl in world. I'm alive."

"I'm on the other side. Don't give it away."

"Well, what do you know," she drawled. "A dick with scruples. Tell it to the seagulls, buster. On me it's just confetti. Run along now, Mr. PI Marlowe, and make that little old phone call you're so anxious about. I'm not restraining you."

She started for the door, but I caught her by the wrist and spun her around. The torn blouse didn't reveal any startling nakedness, merely some skin and part of a brassière. You'd see more on the beach, far more, but you wouldn't see it through a torn blouse.

I must have been leering a little, because she suddenly curled her fingers and tried to claw me.

"I'm no bitch in heat," she said between tight teeth. "Take your paws off me."

I got the other wrist and started to pull her closer. She tried to knee me in the groin, but she was already too close. Then she went limp and pulled her head back and closed her eyes. Her lips opened with a sardonic twist to them. It was a cool evening, maybe even cold down by the water. But it wasn't cold where I was.

After a while she said with a sighing voice that she had to dress for dinner.

I said, "Uh-huh."

After another pause she said it was a long time since a man had unhooked her brassière. We did a slow turn in the direction of one of the twin day beds. They had pink and silver covers on them. The little odd things you notice.

Her eyes were open and quizzical. I studied them one at a time because I was too close to see them together. They seemed well matched.

"Honey," she said softly, "you're awful sweet, but I just don't have the time."

I closed her mouth for her. It seems that a key slid into the door from the outside, but I wasn't paying too close attention. The lock clicked, the door opened, and Mr. Larry Mitchell walked in.

We broke apart. I turned and he looked at me droopy-eyed, six feet one and tough and wiry.

"I thought to check at the office," he said, almost absently. "Twelve B was rented this afternoon, very soon after this was occupied. I got faintly curious, because there are a lot of vacancies here at the moment. So I borrowed the other key. And who is this hunk of beef, baby?"

"She told you not to call her 'baby,' remember?"

If that meant anything to him, he didn't show it. He swung a knotted fist gently at his side.

The girl said: "He's a private eye named Marlowe. Somebody hired him to follow me."

"Did he have to follow you as close as all that? I seem to be intruding on a beautiful friendship."

She jerked away from me and grabbed the gun out of her suitcase. "What we've been talking is money," she told him.

"Always a mistake," Mitchell said. His color was high and his eyes too bright. "Especially in that position. You won't need the gun, honey."

He poked at me with a straight right, very fast and well sprung. I stepped inside it, fast, cool and clever. But the right wasn't his meal ticket. He was a lefty too. I ought to have noticed that at the Union Station in L.A. Trained observer, never miss a detail. I missed him with a right hook and he didn't miss with his left.

It snapped my head back. I went off balance just long enough for him to lunge sideways and lift the gun out of the girl's hand. It seemed to dance through the air and nestle in his left hand.

"Just relax," he said. "I know it sounds corny, but I could drill you and get away with it. I really could."

"Okay," I said thickly. "For fifty bucks a day I don't get shot. That costs seventy-five."

"Please turn around. It would amuse me to look at your wallet."

I lunged for him, gun and all. Only panic could have

made him shoot and he was on his home field and nothing to panic about. But it may be that the girl wasn't so sure. Dimly at the extreme edge of vision I saw her reach for the whiskey bottle on the table.

I caught Mitchell on the side of the neck. His mouth yapped. He hit me somewhere, but it wasn't important. Mine was the better punch, but it didn't win the wrist watch, because at that moment an army mule kicked me square on the back of my brain. I went zooming out over a dark sea and exploded in a sheet of flame.

6

THE FIRST sensation was that if anybody spoke harshly
to me I should burst out crying. The second, that the
room was too small for my head. The front of the head
was a long way from the back, the sides were an enormous distance apart, in spite of which a dull throbbing
beat from temple to temple. Distance means nothing
nowadays.

The third sensation was that somewhere not far off
an insistent whining noise went on. The fourth and last
was that ice water was running down my back. The
cover of a day bed proved that I had been lying on my
face, if I still had one. I rolled over gently and sat up
and a rattling noise ended in a thump. What rattled
and thumped was a knotted towel full of melting ice
cubes. Somebody who loved me very much had put
them on the back of my head. Somebody who loved
me less had bashed in the back of my skull. It could
have been the same person. People have moods.

I got up on my feet and lunged for my hip. The wallet was there in the left pocket, but the flap was unbut-
toned. I went through it. Nothing was gone. It had
yielded its information, but that was no secret any
more. My suitcase stood open on the stand at the foot
of the day bed. So I was home in my own quarters.

I reached a mirror and looked at the face. It seemed

familiar. I went to the door and opened it. The whining
noise was louder. Right in front of me was a fattish
man leaning against the railing. He was a middle-sized
fat man and the fat didn't look flabby. He wore glasses
and large ears under a dull gray felt hat. The collar of
his topcoat was turned up. His hands were in the pockets of his coat. The hair that showed at the sides of his
head was battleship gray. He looked durable. Most fat
men do. The light from the open door behind me
bounced back from his glasses. He had a small pipe in
his mouth, the kind they call a toy bulldog. I was still
foggy but something about him bothered me.

"Nice evening," he said.

"You want something?"

"Looking for a man. You're not him."

"I'm alone in here."

"Right," he said. "Thanks." He turned his back on
me and leaned his stomach against the railing of the
porch.

I went along the porch to the whining noise. The
door of 12C was wide open and the lights were on and
the noise was a vacuum cleaner being operated by a
woman in a green uniform.

I went in and looked the place over. The woman
switched off the vacuum and stared at me. "Something
you wanted?"

"Where's Miss Mayfield?"

She shook her head.

"The lady who had this apartment," I said.

"Oh, that one. She checked out. Half an hour ago."
She switched the vacuum on again. "Better ask at the
office," she yelled through the noise. "This apartment
is on change."

I reached back and shut the door. I followed the
black snake of the vacuum cord over to the wall and
yanked the plug out. The woman in the green uniform
stared at me angrily. I went over and handed her a dollar bill. She looked less angry.

"Just want to phone," I said.

"Ain't you got a phone in your room?"

"Stop thinking," I said. "A dollar's worth."

I went to the phone and lifted it. A girl's voice said: "Office. Your order, please."

"This is Marlowe. I'm very unhappy."

"What? ... Oh yes, Mr. Marlowe. What can we do for you?"

"She's gone. I never even got to talk to her."

"Oh, I'm sorry, Mr. Marlowe," she sounded as if she meant it. "Yes, she left. We couldn't very well—"

"She say where to?"

"She just paid up and left, sir. Quite suddenly. No forwarding address at all."

"With Mitchell?"

"I'm sorry, sir. I didn't see anyone with her."

"You must have seen something. How did she leave?"

"In a taxi. I'm afraid—"

"All right. Thank you." I went back to my apartment.

The middle-sized fat man was sitting comfortably in a chair with his knees crossed.

"Nice of you to drop in," I said. "Anything in particular I could do for you?"

"You could tell me where Larry Mitchell is."

"Larry Mitchell?" I thought it over carefully. "Do I know him?"

He opened a wallet and extracted a card. He struggled to his feet and handed it to me. The card read: Goble and Green, Investigators, 310 Prudence Building, Kansas City, Missouri.

"Must be interesting work, Mr. Goble."

"Don't get funny with me, buster. I get annoyed rather easy."

"Fine. Let's watch you get annoyed. What do you do—bite your mustache?"

"I ain't got no mustache, stupid."

"You could grow one. I can wait."

He got up on his feet much more rapidly this time. He looked down at his fist. Suddenly a gun appeared in his hand. "You ever get pistol-whipped, stupid?"

"Breeze off. You bore me. Mudheads always bore me."

His hand shook and his face turned red. Then he put the gun back in the shoulder holster and wobbled towards the door. "You ain't through with me," he snarled over his shoulder.

I let him have that one. It wasn't worth topping.

7

AFTER a while I went down to the office.

"Well, it didn't work," I said. "Does either one of you happen to have noticed the cabdriver who took her away?"

"Joe Harms," the girl said promptly. "You ought to maybe find him at the stand halfway up Grand. Or you could call the office. A pretty nice guy. He made a pass at me once."

"And missed by from here to Paso Robles," the clerk sneered.

"Oh, I don't know. You didn't seem to be there."

"Yeah," he sighed. "You work twenty hours a day trying to put enough together to buy a home. And by the time you have, fifteen other guys have been smooching your girl."

"Not this one," I said. "She's just teasing you. She glows every time she looks at you."

I went out and left them smiling at each other.

Like most small towns, Esmeralda had one main street from which in both directions its commercial establishments flowed gently for a short block or so and then with hardly a change of mood became streets with houses where people lived. But unlike most small California towns it had no false fronts, no cheesy billboards, no drive-in hamburger joints, no cigar counters or pool-rooms, and no street corner toughs to hang around in front of them. The stores on Grand Street were either old and narrow but not tawdry or else well modernized with plate glass and stainless steel fronts and neon lighting in clear crisp colors. Not everybody in Esmeralda was prosperous, not everybody was happy, not everybody drove a Cadillac, a Jaguar or a Riley, but the percentage of obviously prosperous living was very high, and the stores that sold luxury goods were as neat and expensive-looking as those in Beverly Hills and far less flashy. There was another small difference too. In Esmeralda what was old was also clean and sometimes quaint. In other small towns what is old is just shabby.

I parked midway of the block and the telephone office was right in front of me. It was closed of course, but the entrance was set back and in the alcove which deliberately sacrificed money space to style were two dark green phone booths, like sentry boxes. Across the way was a pale buff taxi, parked diagonally to the curb in slots painted red. A gray-haired man sat in it reading the paper. I crossed to him.

"You Joe Harms?"

He shook his head. "He'll be back after a while. You want a cab?"

"No, thanks."

I walked away from him and looked in at a store window. There was a checked brown and beige sport shirt in the window which reminded me of Larry Mitchell. Walnut brogues, imported tweeds, ties, two or three, and matching shirts for them set out with plenty of room to breathe. Over the store the name of a man who was once a famous athlete. The name was in script, carved and painted in relief against a redwood background.

A telephone jangled and the cabdriver got out of the taxi and went across the sidewalk to answer it. He talked, hung up, got in his cab and backed out of the slot. When he was gone, the street was utterly empty for a minute. Then a couple of cars went by, then a good-looking well dressed colored boy and his prettied up cutie came strolling the block looking in at the windows and chattering. A Mexican in a green bellhop's uniform drove up in somebody's Chrysler New Yorker —it could be his for all I knew—went into the drug-store and came out with a carton of cigarettes. He drove back towards the hotel.

Another beige cab with the name Esmeralda Cab Company tooled around the corner and drifted into the red slot. A big bruiser with thick glasses got out and checked on the wall phone, then got back into his cab and pulled a magazine out from behind his rear-view mirror.

I strolled over to him and he was it. He was coatless and had his sleeves rolled up past the elbows, although this was no Bikini suit weather.

"Yeah. I'm Joe Harms." He stuck a pill in his kisser and lit it with a Ronson.

"Lucille down at the Rancho Descansado thought maybe you'd give me a little information." I leaned against his cab and gave him my big warm smile. I might as well have kicked the curbing.

"Information about what?"

"You picked up a fare this evening from one of their cottages. Number 12C. A tallish girl with reddish hair and a nice shape. Her name's Betty Mayfield but she probably didn't tell you that."

"Mostly they just tell me where they want to go. Quaint, isn't it?" He blew a lungful of smoke at his windshield and watched it flatten out and float around in the cab. "What's the pitch?"

"Girl friend walked out on me. We had a little argument. All my fault. I'd like to tell her I'm sorry."

"Girl friend got a home somewhere?"

"A long way from here."

He knocked ash from his cigarette by flicking his little finger at it still in his mouth.

"Could be she planned it that way. Could be she don't want you to know where she went. Could be you were lucky at that. They can drop the arm on you for shacking up in a hotel in this town. I'll admit it has to be pretty flagrant."

"Could be I'm a liar," I said, and got a business card out of my wallet. He read it and handed it back.

"Better," he said. "Some better. But it's against the company rules. I'm not driving this hack just to build muscle."

"A five interest you? Or is that against the rules too?"

"My old man owns the company. He'd be pretty sore if I was on the chisel. Not that I don't like money."

The phone on the wall jangled. He slid out of the cab and went over to it in about three long strides. I just stood planted, gnawing my lip. He talked and came back and stepped into the cab and was sitting behind the wheel all in one motion.

"Have to blow," he said. "Sorry. I'm kind of behind schedule. Just got back from Del Mar, the seven forty-seven to L.A. makes a flag stop there. Most people from here go that way."

He started his motor and leaned out of the cab to drop his cigarette in the street.

I said, "Thanks."

"For what?" He backed out and was gone.

I looked at my watch again. Time and distance checked. It was all of twelve miles to Del Mar. It would take almost an hour to ferry someone to Del Mar and drop him or her off at the railroad station and turn around and come back. He had told me in his own way. There was no point in telling me at all unless it meant something.

I watched him out of sight and then crossed the street to the booths outside the telephone company's office. I left the booth door open and dropped my dime and dialed the big O.

"I'd like to make a collect call to West Los Angeles, please." I gave her a Bradshaw number. "Person to person, Mr. Clyde Umney. My name is Marlowe and I'm calling from Esmeralda 4-2673, a pay phone."

She got him a lot quicker than it took me to tell her all that. He came on sharp and quick.

"Marlowe? It's about time you reported in. Well— let's have it."

"I'm in San Diego. I've lost her. She slipped away while I was taking a nap."

"I just knew I'd picked a smart cookie," he said unpleasantly.

"It's not as bad as it sounds, Mr. Umney. I have a rough idea where she went."

"Rough ideas are not good enough for me. When I hire a man I expect him to deliver exactly what I order. And just what do you mean by a rough idea?"

"Would it be possible for you to give me some notion of what this is all about, Mr. Umney? I grabbed it off kind of quick on account of meeting the train. Your secretary gave me a lot of personality but very little information. You want me to be happy in my work, don't you, Mr. Umney?"

"I gathered that Miss Vermilyea told you all there is to know," he grumbled. "I am acting at the request of an important law firm in Washington. Their client desires to remain anonymous for the present. All you have to do is trace this party to a stopping place, and by stopping place I do not mean a rest room or a hamburger stand. I mean a hotel, apartment house, or perhaps the home of someone she knows. That's all. How much simpler do you want it?"

"I'm not asking for simplicity, Mr. Umney. I'm asking for background material. Who the girl is, where she came from, what she's supposed to have done to make this job necessary."

"Necessary?" he yapped at me. "Who the hell are you to decide what is necessary? Find that girl, pin her down, and phone me her address. And if you expect to be paid, you better do it damn quick. I'll give you until ten o'clock tomorrow morning. After that I'll make other arrangements."

"Okay, Mr. Umney."

"Where are you exactly and what is your telephone number?"

"I'm just kind of wandering around. I got hit on the head with a whiskey bottle."

"Well, that's too bad," he said acidly. "I presume you had already emptied the bottle."

"Oh it might have been worse, Mr. Umney. It might have been *your* head. I'll call you around ten A.M. at your office. Don't worry about anybody losing anybody. There's two other guys working the same side of the street. One's a local boy named Mitchell and the other is a Kansas City shamus name of Goble. He carries a gun. Well good night, Mr. Umney."

"Hold it!" he roared. "Wait a minute! What does that mean—two other operatives?"

"You asking me what it means? I'm the guy that asked you. Looks like you only got a piece of the job."

"Hold it! Hold it right there!" There was a silence. Then in a steady voice that didn't bluster any more: "I'll call Washington the first thing in the morning, Marlowe. Excuse me if I sounded off. It begins to look as though I am entitled to a little more information about this project."

"Yeah."

"If you make contact again, call me here. At any hour. Any hour at all."

"Yeah."

"Good night, then." He hung up.

I put the phone back on the hook and took a deep breath. My head still ached but the dizziness was gone. I breathed in the cool night air laced with sea fog. I pushed out of the booth and looked across the street. The old guy who had been in the taxi slot when I arrived was back again. I strolled across and asked him how to get to The Glass Room, which was where Mitchell had promised to take Miss Betty Mayfield to dinner—whether she liked it or not. He told me, I thanked him, recrossed the empty street and climbed into my rented car, and started back the way I had come.

It was still possible that Miss Mayfield had grabbed the 7.47 for Los Angeles or some way station. It was a lot more likely that she had not. A cabdriver taking a fare to the station doesn't stick around to watch the fare get on the train. Larry Mitchell wouldn't be that easy to shake. If he had enough on her to make her come to Esmeralda, he had enough on her to keep her there. He knew who I was and what I was doing. He didn't know why, because I didn't know myself. If he had half a brain, and I gave him credit for a good deal more, he would have to assume I could trace her movements as far as a taxi took her. The first guess I was working on was that he would have driven to Del Mar, parked his big Buick somewhere in the shadows, and waited for her taxi to drive up and unload. When it turned around and started back, he would pick her up and drive her back to Esmeralda. The second guess I was working on was that she wouldn't tell him anything he didn't already know. I was a Los Angeles private eye, unknown parties had hired me to follow her, I had done so and then made the mistake of trying to get too close. That would bother him because it suggested he didn't have the field to himself. But if his information, whatever it was, came from a press clipping, he could hardly expect to have it to himself forever. Anybody with enough interest and enough patience could turn it up in time. Anybody with enough reason to hire a private dick probably knew it already. And that in turn meant that whatever kind of bite he planned to put on Betty Mayfield, financial or amatory or both, would have to be put on fast.

A third of a mile down the canyon a small illuminated sign with an arrow pointing seaward said in script *The Glass Room*. The road wound down between cliffside houses with warm lights in the windows, manicured gardens, stucco walls and one or two of fieldstone or brick inset with tiles in the Mexican tradition.

I drove down the last curve of the last hill and the smell of raw seaweed filled my nostrils and the fog-

veiled lights of The Glass Room swelled to amber
brightness and the sound of dance music drifted across
the paved parking lot. I parked with the sea growling
out of sight almost at my feet. There was no attendant.
You just locked your car and went in.

A couple of dozen cars, no more. I looked them
over. One hunch at least had paid off. The Buick
Roadmaster solid top bore a license number I had in
my pocket. It was parked almost at the entrance and
next to it in the very last space near the entrance was a
pale green and ivory Cadillac convertible with oyster-
white leather seats, a plaid traveling rug thrown over
the front seat to keep it dry, and all the gadgets a
dealer could think of, including two enormous spot-
lights with mirrors on them, a radio aerial almost long
enough for a tuna boat, a folding chromium luggage
rack to help out the boot if you wanted to travel far
and in style, a sun visor, a prism reflector to pick up
traffic lights obscured by the visor, a radio with enough
knobs on it for a control panel, a cigarette lighter into
which you dropped your cigarette and it smoked it for
you, and various other trifles which made me wonder
how long it would be before they installed radar,
sound-recording equipment, a bar, and an anti-aircraft
battery.

All this I saw by the light of a clip-on flash. I moved
it to the license holder and the name was Clark Brandon, Hotel Casa del Poniente, Esmeralda, California.

8

THE ENTRANCE lobby was on a balcony which looked down over the bar and a dining room on two levels. A curving carpeted staircase led down to the bar. Nobody was upstairs but the hat-check girl and an elderly party in a phone booth whose expression suggested that nobody better fool with him.

I went down the stairs to the bar and tucked myself in a small curved space that commanded a view of the dance floor. One side of the building was an enormous glass window. Outside of it was nothing but fog, but on a clear night with a moon low over the water it would have been sensational. A three-piece Mexican band was making the kind of music a Mexican band always makes. Whatever they play, it all sounds the same. They always sing the same song, and it always has nice open vowels and a drawn out sugary lilt, and the guy who sings it always strums on a guitar and has a lot to say about *amor, mi corazón,* a lady who is "linda" but very hard to convince, and he always has too long and too oily hair and when he isn't making with the love stuff he looks as if his knife work in an alley would be efficient and economical.

On the dance floor half a dozen couples were throwing themselves around with the reckless abandon of a night watchman with arthritis. Most of them were

44

dancing cheek to cheek, if dancing is the word. The
men wore white tuxedos and the girls wore bright eyes,
ruby lips, and tennis or golf muscles. One couple was
not dancing cheek to cheek. The guy was too drunk to
keep time and the girl was too busy not getting her
pumps walked on to think of anything else. I needn't
have worried about losing Miss Betty Mayfield. She
was there and with Mitchell, but far from happy.
Mitchell's mouth was open, he was grinning, his face
was red and shiny, and his eyes had that glazed look.
Betty was holding her head as far as she could get
away from him without breaking her neck. It was very
obvious that she had had about all of Mr. Larry
Mitchell that she could take.

A Mexican waiter in a short green jacket and white
pants with a green stripe down the side came up and I
ordered a double Gibson and asked if I could have a
club sandwich where I was. He said, *"Muy bien,
señor,"* smiled brightly, and disappeared.

The music stopped, there was desultory clapping.
The orchestra was deeply moved, and played another
number. A dark-haired headwaiter who looked like a
road company Herbert Marshall circulated among the
tables offering his intimate smile and stopping here and
there to polish an apple. Then he pulled out a chair
and sat down opposite a big handsome Irish type character with gray in his hair and just enough of it. He
seemed to be alone. He wore a dark dinner jacket with
a maroon carnation in the lapel. He looked like a nice
guy if you didn't crowd him. At that distance and in
that light I couldn't tell much more, except that if you
did crowd him, you had better be big, fast, tough and
in top condition.

The headwaiter leaned forward and said something
and they both looked towards Mitchell and the Mayfield girl. The captain seemed concerned, the big guy
didn't seem to care much one way or another. The
headwaiter got up and left. The big guy fitted a cigarette into a holder and a waiter popped a lighter at him
as if he had been waiting all evening for the oppor-

tunity. The big guy thanked him without looking up.

My drink came and I grabbed it and drank. The music stopped and stayed stopped. The couples divided and strolled back to their tables. Larry Mitchell still had hold of Betty. He was still grinning. Then he began to pull her close. He put his hand behind her head. She tried to shake him off. He pulled harder and pushed his flushed face down on hers. She struggled but he was too strong for her. He chewed her face some more. She kicked him. He jerked his head up, annoyed.

"Let go of me, you drunken slob," she said breathlessly but very distinctly.

His face got a nasty look. He grabbed her arms hard enough to bruise her and slowly using his strength he pulled her tight against his body and held her there. People looked hard, but nobody moved.

"Whassa matta, baby, you no love poppa no more?" he inquired loudly and thickly.

I didn't see what she did to him with her knee but I could guess and it hurt him. He pushed her away and his face went savage. Then he hauled off and slapped her across the mouth forehand and backhand. The red showed on her skin at once.

She stood quite still. Then in a voice the whole joint could hear she said clearly and slowly: "Next time you do that, Mr. Mitchell—be sure to wear a bullet-proof vest."

She turned and walked away. He just stood there. His face had gone glistening white—whether from pain or rage I couldn't tell. The headwaiter walked softly up to him and murmured something with an inquiring lift of the eyebrow.

Mitchell brought his eyes down and looked at the man. Then without a word he walked right through him and the headwaiter had to stagger out of his way. Mitchell followed Betty, and on the way he bumped a man in a chair and didn't stop to apologize. Betty was sitting down now at a table against the glass wall right next to the big dark guy in the dinner jacket. He

looked at her. He looked at Mitchell. He took his cigarette holder out of his mouth and looked at that. His
face was quite expressionless.

Mitchell reached the table. "You hurt me, sweet-
ness," he said thickly but loudly. "I'm a bad man to
hurt. Catch on? Very bad. Want to apologize?"

She stood up, jerked a wrap off the back of the chair
and faced him.

"Shall I pay the check, Mr. Mitchell—or will you
pay it with what you borrowed from me?"

His hand went back for another swing at her face.
She didn't move. The guy at the next table did. He
came up on his feet in one smooth movement and
grabbed Mitchell's wrist.

"Take it easy, Larry. You've got a skinful." His
voice was cool, almost amused.

Mitchell jerked his wrist loose and spun around.
"Stay out of this, Brandon."

"Delighted, old man. I'm not in it. But you'd better
not slug the lady again. They don't often throw people
out of here—but it could happen."

Mitchell laughed angrily. "Why don't you go spit in
your hat, mister?"

The big man said softly, "Take it easy, Larry, I said.
I won't say it again."

Mitchell glared at him. "Okay, see you later," he
said in a sulky voice. He started off and stopped.
"Much later," he added, half turning. Then he went
out—unsteadily but quickly, looking at nothing.

Brandon just stood there. The girl just stood there.
She looked uncertain about what to do next.

She looked at him. He looked at her. He smiled, just
polite and easygoing, no come-on. She didn't smile
back.

"Anything I could do?" he asked. "Drop you anywhere?" Then he half turned his head. "Oh, Carl."

The headwaiter came up to him quickly.

"No check," Brandon said. "You know, in the circumstances—"

"Please," the girl said sharply. "I don't want other people paying my bills."

He shook his head slowly. "Custom of the house," he said. "Nothing to do with me personally. But may I send you a drink?"

She looked at him some more. He had what it took all right. "Send?" she asked.

He smiled politely. "Well, bring then—if you care to sit down."

And this time he pulled out the chair at his own table. And she sat down. And at that moment, not a second before, the headwaiter signaled the orchestra and they began to play another number.

Mr. Clark Brandon seemed to be the sort of man who got what he wanted without raising his voice.

After a while my club sandwich came. It was nothing to brag about, but eatable. I ate it. I stuck around for half an hour. Brandon and the girl seemed to be doing all right. They were both quiet. After a while they danced. Then I left and sat in the car outside and smoked. She could have seen me although she didn't show it. I knew Mitchell hadn't. He had turned too quickly up the stairs, he had been too mad to see anything.

About ten-thirty, Brandon came out with her and they got into the Cadillac convertible with the top down. I followed it away without trying to hide because the way they went would be the way anybody would go back to the downtown part of Esmeralda. Where they went was to the Casa del Poniente, and Brandon drove down the ramp to the garage.

There was only one thing more to find out. I parked in the side lot and went through the lobby to the house phones.

"Miss Mayfield, please. Betty Mayfield."

"One moment, please"—slight pause—"Oh yes, she just checked in. I'm ringing the room, sir."

Another and much longer pause.

"I'm sorry, Miss Mayfield's room does not answer."

I thanked her and hung up. I beat it out of there fast in case she and Brandon should get off at the lobby.

I went back to my rented chariot, and poked my way along the canyon through the fog to the Rancho Descansado. The cottage where the office was seemed to be locked up and empty. A single hazy light outside showed the position of a night bell. I groped my way up to 12C, tucked the car in the car port, and yawned my way into my room. It was cold and damp and miserable. Someone had been in and taken the striped cover off the day bed and removed the matching pillowcases.

I undressed and put my curly head on the pillow and went to sleep.

9

A TAPPING sound awoke me. It was very light but it was also persistent. I had the feeling that it had been going on a long time and that it had very gradually penetrated my sleep. I rolled over and listened. Somebody tried the door and then the tapping started again. I glanced at my wrist watch. The faint phosphorescence showed it was past three o'clock. I got up on my feet and moved over to my suitcase and reached down into it for the gun. I went over to the door and opened it a crack.

A dark figure in slacks stood there. Some kind of windbreaker also. And a dark scarf knotted around the head. It was a woman.

"What do you want?"

"Let me in—quickly. Don't put any light on."

So it was Betty Mayfield. I pulled the door back and she slid in like a wisp of the fog. I shut the door. I reached for my bathrobe and pulled it on.

"Anybody else outside?" I asked. "There's nobody next door."

"No. I'm alone." She leaned against the wall and breathed quickly. I fumbled my pen flash out of my coat and poked a small beam around and found the heater switch. I shone the little light on her face. She blinked away from it and raised a hand. I put the light down on the floor and trailed it over to the windows and shut them both and lowered and turned the blinds. Then I went back and switched on the lamp.

She let out a gasp, then said nothing. She was still leaning against the wall. She looked as if she needed a drink. I went out to the kitchenette and poured some whiskey into a glass and carried it to her. She waved it away, then changed her mind and grabbed the glass and emptied it.

I sat down and lit a cigarette, the always mechanical reaction that gets so boring when someone else does it. Then I just sat there and looked at her and waited.

Our eyes met across great gulfs of nothing. After a while she reached slowly into the slanted pocket of the windbreaker and pulled out the gun.

"Oh no," I said. "Not that again."

She looked down at the gun. Her lip twitched. She wasn't pointing it anywhere. She pushed herself away from the wall and crossed to lay the gun down at my elbow.

"I've seen it," I said. "We're old friends. Last time I saw it Mitchell had it. So?"

"That's why I knocked you out. I was afraid he would shoot you."

"That would have fouled up all his plans—whatever his plans were."

"Well, I couldn't be sure. I'm sorry. Sorry I hit you."

"Thanks for the ice cubes," I said.

"Aren't you going to look at the gun?"

"I have looked at it."

"I walked all the way over here from the Casa. I'm staying there now. I—moved in this afternoon."

"I know. You took a taxi to the Del Mar station to catch an evening train and then Mitchell picked you up there and drove you back. You had dinner together and danced and there was a little ill-feeling. A man named Clark Brandon took you back to the hotel in his convertible."

She stared. "I didn't see you there," she said finally, in a voice that was thinking of other things.

"I was in the bar. While you were with Mitchell you were too busy getting your face slapped and telling him to wear a bullet-proof vest next time he came around. Then at Brandon's table you sat with your back to me. I left before you did and waited outside."

"I'm beginning to think you *are* a detective," she said quietly. Her eyes went to the gun again. "He never gave it back to me," she said. "Of course I couldn't prove that."

"That means you'd like to be able to."

"It might help a little. It probably wouldn't help quite enough. Not when they found out about me. I guess you know what I'm talking about."

"Sit down and stop grinding your teeth."

She moved slowly to a chair and sat down on the edge and leaned forward. She stared at the floor.

"I know there's something to find out," I said. "Because Mitchell found it out. So I could find it out too—if I tried. Anyone could who knows there is something to find. I don't know at this moment. All I was hired to do was to keep in touch and report back."

She looked up briefly. "And you've done that?"

"I reported in," I said after a pause. "I'd lost contact at the time. I mentioned San Diego. He'd get that from the operator anyway."

"You'd lost contact," she repeated dryly. "He must think a lot of you, whoever he is." Then she bit her lip. "I'm sorry. I didn't mean to say that. I'm trying to make up my mind about something."

"Take your time," I said. "It's only twenty past three A.M."

"Now *you're* sneering."

I looked towards the wall heater. It didn't show a thing, but there seemed to be a lessening of the chill if no more. I decided I needed a drink. I went out to the kitchen and got it. I put it down, poured some more and came back.

She had a small imitation leather folder in her hand now. She showed it to me.

"I have five thousand dollars in American Express

checks in this—one hundred dollar size. How far
would you go for five grand, Marlowe?"

I took a sip of whiskey. I thought about it with a ju-
dicial expression. "Assuming a normal rate of expenses,
that would buy me full time for several months. That is,
if I happened to be for sale."

She tapped on the chair arm with the folder. I could
see that her other hand was almost pulling her kneecap
off.

"You're for sale all right," she said. "And this would
be merely a down payment. I can buy big. I've got
more money than you ever dreamed of. My last husband was so rich that it was pitiful. I got a cool half
million dollars out of him."

She put a hardboiled sneer on her face and gave me
plenty of time to get used to it.

"I take it I wouldn't have to murder anybody?"

"You wouldn't have to murder anybody."

"I don't like the way you say that."

I looked sideways at the gun that I hadn't so far laid
a finger on. She had walked over from the Casa in the
middle of the night to bring it to me. I didn't have to
touch it. I stared at it. I bent over and sniffed it. I still
didn't have to touch it, but I knew I was going to.

"Who's wearing the bullet?" I asked her. The cold in
the room had got into my blood. It ran ice water.

"Just one bullet? How did you know?"

I picked up the gun then. I slipped the magazine
out, looked at it, slipped it back. It snapped home in
the butt.

"Well, it could have been two," I said. "There are six
in the magazine. This gun holds seven. You could jack
one into the chamber and then add another to the
magazine. Of course you could fire the whole supply
and then put six in the magazine."

"We're just talking, aren't we?" she said slowly. "We
don't quite want to say it in plain words."

"All right. Where is he?"

"Lying across a chaise on the balcony of my room.
All the rooms on that side have balconies. They have

concrete walls across them, and the end walls—between the rooms or suites, that is—are slanted outward. I guess a steeplejack or a mountain climber might get around one of the end walls, but not carrying a weight. I'm on the twelfth floor. There's nothing any higher but the penthouse floor." She stopped and frowned, then made a sort of helpless gesture with the hand that had been squeezing her kneecap. "This is going to sound a little corny," she went on. "He could only have got there through my room. And I didn't let him through my room."

"But you're sure he's dead?"

"Quite sure. Quite dead. Stone cold dead. I don't know when it happened. I didn't hear a sound. Something woke me all right. But it wasn't any sound like a shot. Anyhow he was already cold. So I don't know what woke me. And I didn't get up right away. I just lay there, thinking. I didn't go back to sleep, so after a while I put the light on and got up and walked around and smoked. Then I noticed the fog was gone and it was moonlight. Not down on the ground, but up there on my floor. I could still see fog down below when I went out on the balcony. It was damned cold. The stars seemed enormous. I stood there near the wall for quite a while before I even saw him. I guess that sounds pretty corny too—or pretty unlikely. I can't imagine the police taking it very seriously—even at first. And afterwards—well, just take it this way. I haven't a chance in a million—unless I get help."

I stood up, tossed down what whiskey was left in the glass and walked over to her.

"Let me tell you two or three things. First off, you're not taking this with normal reactions. You're not icy cool, but you're too cool. No panic, no hysteria, no nothing. You're fatalistic. Next, I heard the entire conversation between you and Mitchell this afternoon. I took those bulbs out"—I pointed to the wall heater—"and used a stethoscope against the partition at the back. What Mitchell had on you was a knowledge of who you were, and that knowledge was something that

if published could drive you into another switch of
names and another dodge to some other town somewhere. You said you were the luckiest girl in the world
because you were alive. Now a man is dead on your
balcony, shot with your gun, and the man of course is
Mitchell. Right?"

She nodded. "Yes, it's Larry."

"And you didn't kill him, you say. And the cops
would hardly believe that even at first, you say. And
later on not at all. My guess is that you've been there
before."

She was still looking up at me. She came slowly to
her feet. Our faces were close, we stared hard into each
other's eyes. It didn't mean a thing.

"Half a million dollars is a lot of money, Marlowe.
You're not too hard to take. There are places in the
world where you and I could have a beautiful life. In
one of those tall apartment houses along the ocean
front in Rio. I don't know how long it would last, but
things can always be arranged, don't you think?"

I said: "What a lot of different girls you are. Now
you're making like a moll. When I first saw you, you
were a quiet well-bred little lady. You didn't like
dreamboats like Mitchell making a pitch at you. Then
you bought yourself a pack of cigarettes and smoked
one as if you hated it. Then you let him cuddle you—
after you got down here. Then you tore your blouse at
me ha, ha, ha, cynical as a Park Avenue pet after her
butter and egg man goes home. Then you let me
cuddle you. Then you cracked me on the head with a
whiskey bottle. Now you're talking about a beautiful
life in Rio. Which one of you would have her head on
the next pillow when I woke up in the morning?"

"Five thousand dollars down. And a lot more to
come. The police wouldn't give you five toothpicks. If
you think different, you have a telephone."

"What do I do for the five grand?"

She let her breath out slowly as if a crisis was past.
"The hotel is built almost on the edge of the cliff. At
the foot of the wall there's only a narrow walk, very

narrow. Below the cliffs are rocks and the sea. It's almost high tide. My balcony hangs right over all that."

I nodded. "Are there fire stairs?"

"From the garage. They start just beside the basement elevator landing, which is up two or three steps from the garage floor. But it's a long hard climb."

"For five grand I'd climb it in a diver's suit. Did you come out through the lobby?"

"Fire stairs. There's an all night man in the garage but he was asleep in one of the cars."

"You said Mitchell is lying on a chaise. Is there a lot of blood?"

She winced. "I—I didn't notice. I suppose there must be."

"You didn't notice? You went near enough to find out he was stone cold dead. Where was he shot?"

"Nowhere that I saw. It must have been under him."

"Where was the gun?"

"It was lying on the floor of the porch—beside his hand."

"Which hand?"

She widened her eyes slightly. "Does it matter? I don't know which hand. He's sort of lying across the chaise with his head hanging on one side and his legs on the other. Do we have to keep on talking about it?"

"All right," I said. "I don't know a damn thing about the tides and currents around here. He might wash up on the beach tomorrow and he might not show up for two weeks. Assuming, of course, we bring it off. If it's a long time they may not even find out he was shot. Then I guess there's some possibility that he won't be found at all. Not much, but some. There are barracuda in these waters, and other things."

"You certainly do a thorough job of making it revolting," she said.

"Well, I had a running start. Also I was thinking if there was any chance of suicide. Then we'd have to put the gun back. He was left-handed, you know. That's why I wanted to know which hand."

"Oh. Yes, he was left-handed. You're right. But not suicide. Not that smirking, self-satisfied gentleman."

"Sometimes a man kills the dearest thing he loves, they say. Couldn't it be himself?"

"Not this character," she said briefly and finally. "If we are very lucky, they will probably think he fell off the balcony. God knows he was drunk enough. And by that time I'll be in South America. My passport is still valid."

"In what name is your passport?"

She reached out and drew her fingertips down my cheek. "You'll know all about me soon enough. Don't be impatient. You'll know all the intimate things about me. Can't you wait a little?"

"Yeah. Start getting intimate with those American Express checks. We have another hour or two of darkness and more than that of fog. You play with the checks while I get dressed."

I reached into my jacket and gave her a fountain pen. She sat down near the light and began to sign them with the second signature. Her tongue peeped out between her teeth. She wrote slowly and carefully. The name she wrote was Elizabeth Mayfield.

So the switch of names had been planned before she left Washington.

While I dressed I wondered if she was really foolish enough to think I'd help her dispose of a body.

I carried the glasses out to the kitchenette and scooped the gun up on the way. I let the swing door close and slipped the gun and the magazine into the tray under the broiler of the stove. I rinsed out the glasses and wiped them off. I went back into the living room and threw my clothes on. She didn't even look at me.

She went on signing the checks. When she had finished, I took the folder of checks and flipped them over one by one, checking the signatures. The big money meant nothing to me. I shoved the folder into my pocket, put the lamp out and moved to the door. I opened it and she was beside me. She was close beside me.

"Sneak out," I said. "I'll pick you up on the highway just above where the fence ends."

She faced me and leaned a little towards me. "Can I trust you?" she asked softly.

"Up to a point."

"You're honest at least. What happens if we don't get away with it? If somebody reported a shot, if he has been found, if we walk in on that and the place is full of policemen?"

I just stood there with my eyes on her face and didn't answer her.

"Just let me guess," she said very softly and slowly. "You'll sell me out fast. And you won't have any five thousand dollars. Those checks will be old newspaper. You won't dare cash a single one of them."

I still didn't say anything.

"You son of a bitch." She didn't raise her voice even a semitone. "Why did I ever come to you?"

I took her face between my hands and kissed her on the lips. She pulled away.

"Not for that," she said. "Certainly not for that. And one more small point. It's terribly small and unimportant, I know. I've had to learn that. From expert teachers. Long hard painful lessons and a lot of them. It just happens that I really didn't kill him."

"Maybe I believe you."

"Don't bother to try," she said. "Nobody else will."

She turned and slid along the porch and down the steps. She flitted off through the trees. In thirty feet the fog hid her.

I locked up and got into the rent car and drove it down the silent driveway past the closed office with the light over the night bell. The whole place was hard asleep, but trucks were rumbling up through the canyon with building materials and oil and the big closed up jobs with and without trailers, full of anything and everything that a town needs to live on. The fog lights were on and the trucks were slow and heavy up the hill.

Fifty yards beyond the gate she stepped out of the shadows at the end of the fence and climbed in. I switched on my headlights. Somewhere out on the water a foghorn was moaning. Upstairs in the clear reaches of the sky a formation of jets from North Island went over with a whine and a whoosh and a bang of the shock wave and were gone in less time than it took me to pull the lighter out of the dash and light a cigarette.

The girl sat motionless beside me, looking straight ahead and not speaking. She wasn't seeing the fog or the back of a truck we were coming up behind. She wasn't seeing anything. She was just sitting there frozen in one position, stony with despair, like somebody on the way to be hanged.

Either that or she was the best little scene stealer I had come across in a long long time.

10

THE CASA DEL PONIENTE was set on the edge of the cliffs in about seven acres of lawn and flower beds, with a central patio on the sheltered side, tables set out behind a glass screen, and a trellised walk leading through the middle of it to an entrance. There was a bar on one side, a coffee shop on the other, and at each end of the building blacktop parking lots partly hidden behind six-foot hedges of flowering shrubs. The parking lots had cars in them. Not everyone bothered to use the basement garage, although the damp salt air down there is hard on chromium.

I parked in a slot near the garage ramp and the sound of the ocean was very close and you could feel the drifting spray and smell it and taste it. We got out and moved over to the garage entrance. A narrow raised walk edged the ramp. A sign hung midway of the entrance said: Descend in Low Gear. Sound Horn. The girl grabbed me by the arm and stopped me.

"I'm going in by the lobby. I'm too tired to climb the stairs."

"Okay. No law against it. What's the room number?"

"Twelve twenty-four. What do we get if we're caught?"

"Caught doing what?"

"You know what. Putting—putting it over the balcony wall. Or somewhere."

"I'd get staked out on an anthill. I don't know about you. Depends what else they have on you."

"How can you talk like that before breakfast?"

She turned and walked away quickly. I started down the ramp. It curved as they all do and then I could see a glassed-in cubbyhole of an office with a hanging light in it. A little farther down and I could see that it was empty. I listened for sounds of somebody doing a little work on a car, water in a washrack, steps, whistling, any little noise to indicate where the night man was and what he was doing. In a basement garage you can hear a very small noise indeed. I heard nothing.

I went on down and was almost level with the upper end of the office. Now by stooping I could see the shallow steps up into the basement elevator lobby. There was a door marked: To Elevator. It had glass panels and I could see light beyond it, but little else.

I took three more steps and froze. The night man was looking right at me. He was in a big Packard sedan in the back seat. The light shone on his face and he wore glasses and the light shone hard on the glasses. He was leaning back comfortably in the corner of the car. I stood there and waited for him to move. He didn't move. His head was against the car cushions. His mouth was open. I had to know why he didn't move. He might be just pretending to be asleep until I got out of sight. When that happened he would beat it across to the phone and call the office.

Then I thought that was silly. He wouldn't have come on the job until evening and he couldn't know all the guests by sight. The sidewalk that bordered the ramp was there to walk on. It was almost 4 A.M. In an hour or so it would begin to get light. No hotel prowler would come around that late.

I walked straight over to the Packard and looked in on him. The car was shut up tight, all windows. The man didn't move. I reached for the door handle and tried to open the door without noise. He still didn't move. He looked like a very light colored man. He also looked asleep and I could hear him snoring even before I got the door open. Then I got it full in the face —the honeyed reek of well-cured marijuana. The guy was out of circulation, he was in the valley of peace, where time is slowed to a standstill, where the world is all colors and music. And in a couple of hours from now he wouldn't have a job, even if the cops didn't grab him and toss him into the deep freeze.

I shut the car door again and crossed to the glass-paneled door. I went through into a small bare elevator lobby with a concrete floor and two blank elevator doors and beside them, opening on a heavy door closer, the fire stairs. I pulled that open and started up. I went slowly. Twelve stories and a basement take a lot of stairs. I counted the fire doors as I passed them because they were not numbered. They were heavy and solid and gray like the concrete of the steps. I was sweating and out of breath when I pulled open the door to the twelfth-floor corridor. I prowled along to Room 1224 and tried the knob. It was locked, but almost at once the door was opened, as if she had been waiting just behind it. I went in past her and flopped into a chair and waited to get some breath back. It was a big airy room with french windows opening on a balcony. The double bed had been slept in or arranged to look that way. Odds and ends of clothing on chairs, toilet articles on the dresser, luggage. It looked about twenty bucks a day, single.

She turned the night latch in the door. "Have any trouble?"

"The night man was junked to the eyes. Harmless as a kitten." I heaved myself out of the chair and started across to the french doors.

"Wait!" she said sharply. I looked back at her. "It's no use," she said. "Nobody could do a thing like that."

I stood there and waited.

"I'd rather call the police," she said. "Whatever it means for me."

"That's a bright idea," I said. "Why ever didn't we think of it before?"

"You'd better leave," she said. "There's no need for you to be mixed up in it."

I didn't say anything. I watched her eyes. She could hardly keep them open. It was either delayed shock or some kind of dope. I didn't know which.

"I swallowed two sleeping pills," she said, reading my mind. "I just can't take any more trouble tonight. Go away from here. Please. When I wake I'll call room service. When the waiter comes I'll get him out on the balcony somehow and he'll find—whatever he'll find. And I won't know a damn thing about it." Her tongue was getting thick. She shook herself and rubbed hard against her temples. "I'm sorry about the money. You'll have to give it back to me, won't you?"

I went over close to her. "Because if I don't you'll tell them the whole story?"

"I'll have to," she said drowsily. "How can I help it? They'll get it out of me. I'm—I'm too tired to fight any more."

I took hold of her arm and shook her. Her head wobbled. "Quite sure you only took two capsules?"

She blinked her eyes open. "Yes. I never take more than two."

"Then listen. I'm going out there and have a look at him. Then I'm going back to the Rancho. I'm going to keep your money. Also I have your gun. Maybe it can't be traced to me but— Wake up! Listen to me!" Her head was rolling sideways again. She jerked straight and her eyes widened, but they looked dull and withdrawn. "Listen. If it can't be traced to you, it certainly can't be traced to me. I'm working for a lawyer and my assignment is you. The traveler's checks and the gun will go right where they belong. And your story to the cops won't be worth a wooden nickel. All it will do is help to hang you. Understand that?"

"Ye-es," she said. "And I don't g-give a damn."

"That's not you talking. It's the sleeping medicine."

She sagged forward and I caught her and steered her

over to the bed. She flopped on it any old way. I pulled
her shoes off and spread a blanket over her and tucked
her in. She was asleep at once. She began to snore. I
went into the bathroom and groped around and found
a bottle of Nembutal on the shelf. It was almost full. It
had a prescription number and a date on it. The date
was a month old, the drugstore was in Baltimore. I
dumped the yellow capsules out into my palm and
counted them. There were forty-seven and they almost
filled the bottle. When they take them to kill themselves,
they take them all—except what they spill, and they
nearly always spill some. I put the pills back in the
bottle and put the bottle in my pocket.

I went back and looked at her again. The room was
cold. I turned the radiator on, not too much. And finally at long last I opened the french doors and went
out on the balcony. It was as cold as hell out there.
The balcony was about twelve by fourteen feet, with a
thirty-inch wall across the front and a low iron railing
sprouting out of that. You could jump off easy enough,
but you couldn't possibly fall off accidentally. There
were two aluminum patio chaises with padded cushions, two armchairs of the same type. The dividing
wall to the left stuck out the way she had told me. I
didn't think even a steeplejack could get around the
projection without climbing tackle. The wall at the
other end rose sheer to the edge of what must be one of
the penthouse terraces.

Nobody was dead on either of the chaises, nor on
the floor of the balcony, nor anywhere at all. I exam-
ined them for traces of blood. No blood. No blood on
the balcony. I went along the safety wall. No blood. No
signs of anything having been heaved over. I stood
against the wall and held on to the metal railing and
leaned out as far as I could lean. I looked straight down
the face of the wall to the ground. Shrubs grew close to
it, then a narrow strip of lawn, then a flagstone foot-
path, then another strip of lawn and then a heavy fence
with more shrubs growing against that. I estimated the

distance. At that height it wasn't easy, but it must have been at least thirty-five feet. Beyond the fence the sea creamed on some half-submerged rocks.

Larry Mitchell was about half an inch taller than I was but weighed about fifteen pounds less, at a rough guess. The man wasn't born who could heave a hundred and seventy-five pound body over that railing and far enough out to fall into the ocean. It was barely possible that a girl wouldn't realize that, just barely possible, about one tenth of one per cent possible.

I opened the french door and went through and shut it and crossed to stand beside the bed. She was still sound asleep. She was still snoring. I touched her cheek with the back of my hand. It was moist. She moved a little and mumbled. Then she sighed and settled her head into the pillow. No stertorous breathing, no deep stupor, no coma, and therefore no overdose.

She had told me the truth about one thing, and about damned little else.

I found her bag in the top drawer of the dresser. It had a zipper pocket at the back. I put her folder of traveler's checks in it and looked through it for information. There was some crisp folding money in the zipper pocket, a Santa Fe timetable, the folder her ticket had been in and the stub of the railroad ticket and the Pullman reservation. She had had Bedroom E on Car 19, Washington, D.C., to San Diego, California. No letters, nothing to identify her. That would be locked up in the luggage. In the main part of the bag was what a woman carries, a lipstick, a compact, a change purse, some silver, and a few keys on a ring with a tiny bronze tiger hanging from it. A pack of cigarettes that seemed just about full but had been opened. A matchbook with one match used. Three handkerchiefs with no initials, a packet of emery boards, a cuticle knife, and some kind of eyebrow stuff, a comb in a leather case, a little round jar of nail polish, a tiny address book. I pounced on that. Blank, not used at all. Also in the bag were a pair of sun glasses with spangled rims in a case, no name on the case; a fountain pen, a small gold pencil, and that was all. I put the bag back where I had found it. I went over to the desk for a piece of hotel stationery and an envelope.

I used the hotel pen to write: "Dear Betty: So sorry I couldn't stay dead. Will explain tomorrow. Larry."

I sealed the note in the envelope, wrote *Miss Betty Mayfield* on it, and dropped it where it might be if it had been pushed under the door.

I opened the door, went out, shut the door, and went back to the fire stairs, then said out loud: "The hell with it," and rang for the elevator. It didn't come. I rang again and kept on ringing. Finally it came up and a sleepy-eyed young Mexican opened the doors and yawned at me, then grinned apologetically. I grinned back and said nothing.

There was nobody at the desk, which faced the elevators. The Mexican parked himself in a chair and went back to sleep before I had taken six steps. Everybody was sleepy but Marlowe. He works around the clock, and doesn't even collect.

I drove back to the Rancho Descansado, saw nobody awake there, looked longingly at the bed, but packed my suitcase—with Betty's gun in the bottom of it—put twelve bucks in an envelope and on the way out put that through the slot in the office door, with my room key.

I drove to San Diego, turned the rent car in, and ate breakfast at a joint across from the station. At seven-fifteen I caught the two-car diesel job that makes the run to L.A. nonstop and pulls in at exactly 10 A.M.

I rode home in a taxi and shaved and showered and ate a second breakfast and glanced through the morning paper. It was near on eleven o'clock when I called the office of Mr. Clyde Umney, the lawyer.

He answered himself. Maybe Miss Vermilyea hadn't got up yet.

"This is Marlowe. I'm home. Can I drop around?"

"Did you find her?"

"Yeah. Did you call Washington?"

"Where is she?"

"I'd like to tell you in person. Did you call Washington?"

"I'd like your information first. I have a very busy day ahead." His voice was brittle and lacked charm.

"I'll be there in half an hour." I hung up fast and called the place where my Olds was.

11

THERE ARE almost too many offices like Clyde Umney's office. It was paneled in squares of combed plywood set at right angles one to the other to make a checkerboard effect. The lighting was indirect, the carpeting wall to wall, the furniture blond, the chairs comfortable, and the fees probably exorbitant. The metal window frames opened outward and there was a small but neat parking lot behind the building, and every slot in it had a name painted on a white board. For some reason Clyde Umney's stall was vacant, so I used it. Maybe he had a chauffeur drive him to his office. The building was four stories high, very new, and occupied entirely by doctors and lawyers.

When I entered, Miss Vermilyea was just fixing herself for a hard day's work by touching up her platinum blond coiffure. I thought she looked a little the worse for wear. She put away her hand mirror and fed herself a cigarette.

"Well, well. Mr. Hard Guy in person. To what may we attribute this honor?"

"Umney's expecting me."

"*Mister* Umney to you, buster."

"Boydie-boy to you, sister."

She got raging in an instant. "Don't call me 'sister,' you cheap gumshoe!"

"Then don't call me buster, you very expensive secretary. What are you doing tonight? And don't tell me you're going out with four sailors again."

The skin around her eyes turned whiter. Her hand crisped into a claw around a paperweight. She just didn't heave it at me. "You son of a bitch!" she said somewhat pointedly. Then she flipped a switch on her talk box and said to the voice: "Mr. Marlowe is here, Mr. Umney."

Then she leaned back and gave me the look. "I've got friends who could cut you down so small you'd need a stepladder to put your shoes on."

"Somebody did a lot of hard work on that one," I said. "But hard work's no substitute for talent."

Suddenly we both burst out laughing. The door opened and Umney stuck his face out. He gestured me in with his chin, but his eyes were on the platinum girl.

I went in and after a moment he closed the door and went behind his enormous semicircular desk, with a green leather top and just piles and piles of important documents on it. He was a dapper man, very carefully dressed, too short in the legs, too long in the nose, too sparse in the hair. He had limpid brown eyes which, for a lawyer, looked very trustful.

"You making a pass at my secretary?" he asked me in a voice that was anything but limpid.

"Nope. We were just exchanging pleasantries."

I sat down in the customer's chair and looked at him with something approaching politeness.

"She looked pretty mad to me." He squatted in his executive vice-president type chair and made his face tough.

"She's booked up for three weeks," I said. "I couldn't wait that long."

"Just watch your step, Marlowe. Lay off. She's private property. She wouldn't give you the time of day. Besides being a lovely piece of female humanity, she's as smart as a whip."

"You mean she can type and take dictation as well?"

"As well as what?" He reddened suddenly. "I've taken enough lip from you. Just watch your step. Very carefully. I have enough influence around this town to hang a red light on you. Now let me have your report and make it short and to the point."

"You talk to Washington yet?"

"Never mind what I did or didn't do. I want your report as of right now. The rest is my business. What's the present location of the King girl?" He reached for a nice sharp pencil and a nice clean pad. Then he dropped the pencil and poured himself a glass of water from a black and silver thermos jug.

"Let's trade," I said. "You tell me why you want her found and I'll tell you where she is."

"You're my employee," he snapped. "I don't have to give you any information whatsoever." He was still tough but beginning to shred a little around the edge.

"I'm your employee if I want to be, Mr. Umney. No check has been cashed, no agreement has been made."

"You accepted the assignment. You took an advance."

"Miss Vermilyea gave me a check for two hundred and fifty as an advance, and another check for two hundred for expenses. But I didn't bank them. Here they are." I took the two checks out of my pocketbook and laid them on the desk in front of him. "Better keep them until you make up your mind whether you want an investigator or a yes man, and until I make up my mind whether I was offered a job or was being suckered into a situation I knew nothing about."

He looked down at the checks. He wasn't happy. "You've already had expenses," he said slowly.

"That's all right, Mr. Umney. I had a few dollars saved up—and the expenses are deductible. Also I've had fun."

"You're pretty stubborn, Marlowe."

"I guess, but I have to be in my business. Otherwise I wouldn't be in business. I told you the girl was being blackmailed. Your Washington friends must know why.

If she's a crook, fine. But I have to get told. And I have an offer you can't match."

"For more money you are willing to switch sides?" he asked angrily. "That would be unethical."

I laughed. "So I've got ethics now. Maybe we're getting somewhere."

He took a cigarette out of a box and lit it with a pot-bellied lighter that matched the thermos and the pen set.

"I still don't like your attitude," he growled. "Yesterday I didn't know any more than you did. I took it for granted that a reputable Washington law firm would not ask me to do anything against legal ethics. Since the girl could have been arrested without difficulty, I assumed it was some sort of domestic mix-up, a runaway wife or daughter, or an important but reluctant witness who was already outside the jurisdiction where she could be subpoenaed. That was just guessing. This morning things are a little different."

He got up and walked to the big window and turned the slats of the blinds enough to keep the sun off his desk. He stood there smoking, looking out, then came back to the desk and sat down again.

"This morning," he went on slowly and with a judicious frown, "I talked to my Washington associates and I am informed that the girl was confidential secretary to a rich and important man—I'm not told his name—and that she absconded with certain important and dangerous papers from his private files. Papers that might be damaging to him if made public. I'm not told in what way. Perhaps he has been fudging his tax returns. You never know these days."

"She took this stuff to blackmail him?"

Umney nodded. "That is the natural assumption. They had no value to her otherwise. The client, Mr. A we will call him, didn't realize that the girl had left until she was already in another state. He then checked his files and found that some of his material was gone. He was reluctant to go to the police. He expects the girl to go far enough away to feel safe and from that

point to start negotiations with him for the return of
the material at a heavy price. He wants to peg her
down somewhere without her knowing it, walk in and
catch her off balance and especially before she contacts
some sharp lawyer, of whom I regret to say there are
far too many, and with the sharp lawyer works out a
scheme that would make her safe from prosecution.
Now you tell me someone is blackmailing her. On what
grounds?"

"If your story stood up, it could be because he is in
a position to spoil her play," I said. "Maybe he knows
something that could hang a pinch on her without
opening up the other box of candy."

"You say if the story stood up," he snapped. "What
do you mean by that?"

"It's as full of holes as a sink strainer. You're being
fed a line, Mr. Umney. Where would a man keep material like the important papers you mention—if he had
to keep them at all? Certainly not where a secretary
could get them. And unless he missed the stuff before
she left, how did he get her followed to the train? Next,
although she took a ticket to California, she could have
got off anywhere. Therefore she would have to be
watched on the train, and if that was done, why did
someone need me to pick her up here? Next, this, as
you tell it, would be a job for a large agency with na-
tion-wide connections. It would be idiotic to take a
chance on one man. I lost her yesterday. I could lose
her again. It takes a bare minimum of six operatives to
do a standard tail job in any sizable place, and that's
just what I mean—a bare minimum. In a really big city
you'd need a dozen. An operative has to eat and sleep
and change his shirt. If he's tailing by car he has to be
able to drop a man while he finds a place to park. Department stores and hotels may have half a dozen en-
trances. But all this girl does is hang around Union
Station here for three hours in full view of everybody.
And all your friends in Washington do is mail you a
picture, call you on the phone, and then go back to
watching television."

"Very clear," he said. "Anything else?" His face was deadpan now.

"A little. Why—if she didn't expect to be followed—would she change her name? Why if she did expect to be followed would she make it so easy? I told you two other guys were working the same side of the street. One is a Kansas City private detective named Goble. He was in Esmeralda yesterday. He knew just where to go. Who told him? I had to follow her and bribe a taxi driver to use his R/T outfit to find out where her cab was going so that I wouldn't lose her. So why was I hired?"

"We'll come to that," Umney said curtly. "Who was the other party you say was working the same side of the street?"

"A playboy named Mitchell. He lives down there. He met the girl on the train. He made a reservation for her in Esmeralda. They're just like that"—I held up two touching fingers—"except that she hates his guts. He's got something on her and she is afraid of him. What he has on her is a knowledge of who she is, where she came from, what happened to her there, and why she is trying to hide under another name. I overheard enough to know that, but not enough to give me exact information."

Umney said acidly: "Of course the girl was covered on the train. Do you think you are dealing with idiots? You were nothing more than a decoy—to determine whether she had any associates. On your reputation— such as it is—I relied on you to grandstand just enough to let her get wise to you. I guess you know what an open shadow is."

"Sure. One that deliberately lets the subject spot him, then shake him, so that another shadow can pick him up when he thinks he is safe."

"You were it." He grinned at me contemptuously. "But you still haven't told me where she is."

I didn't want to tell him, but I knew I'd have to. I had up to a point accepted the assignment, and giving him back his money was only a move to force some information out of him.

I reached across the desk and picked up the $250 check. "I'll take this as payment in full, expenses included. She is registered as Miss Betty Mayfield at the Casa del Poniente in Esmeralda. She is loaded with money. But of course your expert organization must know all this already."

I stood up. "Thanks for the ride, Mr. Umney."

I went out and shut his door. Miss Vermilyea looked up from a magazine. I heard a faint muffled click from somewhere in her desk.

"I'm sorry I was rude to you," I said. "I didn't get enough sleep last night."

"Forget it. It was a stand-off. With a little practice I might get to like you. You're kind of cute in a low down sort of way."

"Thanks," I said and moved to the door. I wouldn't say she looked exactly wistful, but neither did she look as hard to get as a controlling interest in General Motors.

I turned back and closed the door.

"I guess it's not raining tonight, is it? There was something we might have discussed over a drink, if it had been a rainy night. And if you had not been too busy."

She gave me a cool amused look. "Where?"

"That would be up to you."

"Should I drop by your place?"

"It would be damn nice of you. That Fleetwood might help my credit standing."

"I wasn't exactly thinking of that."

"Neither was I."

"About six-thirty perhaps. And I'll take good care of my nylons."

"I was hoping you would."

Our glances locked. I went out quickly.

12

AT HALF PAST six the Fleetwood purred to the front door and I had it open when she came up the steps. She was hatless. She wore a flesh-colored coat with the collar turned up against her platinum hair. She stood in the middle of the living room and looked around casually. Then she slipped the coat off with a lithe movement and threw it on the davenport and sat down.

"I didn't really think you'd come," I said.

"No. You're the shy type. You knew darned well I'd come. Scotch and soda, if you have it."

"I have it."

I brought the drinks and sat down beside her, but not close enough for it to mean anything. We touched glasses and drank.

"Would you care to go to Romanoff's for dinner?"

"And then what?"

"Where do you live?"

"West Los Angeles. A house on a quiet old street. It happens to belong to me. I asked you, and then what, remember?"

"That would be up to you, naturally."

"I thought you were a tough guy. You mean I don't have to pay for my dinner?"

"I ought to slap your face for that crack."

She laughed suddenly and stared at me over the edge of her glass.

"Consider it slapped. We had each other a bit wrong. Romanoff's could wait a while, couldn't it?"

"We could try West Los Angeles first."

"Why not here?"

"I guess this will make you walk out on me. I had a dream here once, a year and a half ago. There's still a shred of it left. I'd like it to stay in charge."

She stood up quickly and grabbed her coat. I managed to help her on with it.

"I'm sorry," I said. "I should have told you before."

She swung around with her face close to mine, but I didn't touch her.

"Sorry that you had a dream and kept it alive? I've had dreams too, but mine died. I didn't have the courage to keep them alive."

"It's not quite like that. There was a woman. She was rich. She thought she wanted to marry me. It wouldn't have worked. I'll probably never see her again. But I remember."

"Let's go," she said quietly. "And let's leave the memory in charge. I only wish I had one worth remembering."

On the way down to the Cadillac I didn't touch her either. She drove beautifully. When a woman is a really good driver she is just about perfect.

13

THE HOUSE was on a curving quiet street between San Vincente and Sunset Boulevard. It was set far back and had a long driveway and the entrance to the house was at the back with a small patio in front of it. She unlocked the door and switched on lights all over the house and then disappeared without a word. The living room had nicely mixed furniture and a feeling of comfort. I stood waiting until she came back with two tall glasses. She had taken her coat off.

"You've been married, of course," I said.

"It didn't take. I got this house and some money out of it, but I wasn't gunning for anything. He was a nice guy, but we were wrong for each other. He's dead now—plane crash—he was a jet pilot. Happens all the time. I know a place between here and San Diego that is full of girls who were married to jet pilots when they were alive."

I took a single sip of my drink and put it down.

I lifted her glass out of her hand and put it down too.

"Remember yesterday morning when you told me to stop looking at your legs?"

"I seem to remember."

"Try and stop me now."

I took hold of her and she came into my arms without a word. I picked her up and carried her and somehow found the bedroom. I put her down on the bed. I peeled her skirt up until I could see the white thighs above her long beautiful nylon-clad legs. Suddenly she reached up and pulled my head down against her breast.

"Beast! Could we have a little less light?"

I went to the door and switched the light off in the room. There was still a glow from the hall. When I turned she was standing by the bed as naked as Aphrodite, fresh from the Aegean. She stood there proudly and without either shame or enticement.

"Damn it," I said, "when I was young you could undress a girl slowly. Nowadays she's in the bed while you're struggling with your collar button."

"Well, struggle with your goddam collar button."

She pulled the bedcovers back and lay on the bed shamelessly nude. She was just a beautiful naked woman completely unashamed of being what she was.

"Satisfied with my legs?" she asked.

I didn't answer.

"Yesterday morning," she said, half dreamily, "I said there was something about you I liked—you didn't paw—and something I didn't like. Know what it was?"

"No."

"That you didn't make me do this then."

"Your manner hardly encouraged it."

"You're supposed to be a detective. Please put out all the lights now."

Then very soon in the dark she was saying, "Darling, darling, darling" in that very special tone of voice a woman uses only in those special moments. Then a slow gentle relaxing, a peace, a quietness.

"Still satisfied with my legs?" she asked dreamily.

"No man ever would be. They would haunt him, no matter how many times he made love to you."

"You bastard. You complete bastard. Come closer."

She put her head on my shoulder and we were very close now.

"I don't love you," she said.

"Why would you? But let's not be cynical about it. There are sublime moments—even if they are only moments."

I felt her tight and warm against me. Her body surged with vitality. Her beautiful arms held me tight.

And again in the darkness that muted cry, and then again the slow quiet peace.

"I hate you," she said with her mouth against mine. "Not for this, but because perfection never comes twice and with us it came too soon. And I'll never see you again and I don't want to. It would have to be forever or not at all."

"And you acted like a hardboiled pick-up who had seen too much of the wrong side of life."

"So did you. And we were both wrong. And it's useless. Kiss me harder."

Suddenly she was gone from the bed almost without sound or movement.

After a little while the light went on in the hallway and she stood in the door in a long wrapper.

"Goodbye," she said calmly. "I'm calling a taxi for you. Wait out in front for it. You won't see me again."

"What about Umney?"

"A poor frightened jerk. He needs someone to bolster his ego, to give him a feeling of power and conquest. I give it to him. A woman's body is not so sacred that it can't be used—especially when she has already failed at love."

She disappeared. I got up and put my clothes on and listened before I went out. I heard nothing. I called out, but there was no answer. When I reached the sidewalk in front of the house the taxi was just pulling up. I looked back. The house seemed completely dark.

No one lived there. It was all a dream. Except that someone had called the taxi. I got into it and was driven home.

14

I LEFT Los Angeles and hit the superhighway that now bypassed Oceanside. I had time to think.

From Los Angeles to Oceanside were eighteen miles of divided six-lane superhighway dotted at intervals with the carcasses of wrecked, stripped, and abandoned cars tossed against the high bank to rust until they were hauled away. So I started thinking about why I was going back to Esmeralda. The case was all backwards and it wasn't my case anyway. Usually a PI gets a client who, for too little money, wants too much information. You get it or you don't, depending on circumstances. The same with your fee. But once in a while you get the information and too much else, including a story about a body on a balcony which wasn't there when you went to look. Common sense says go home and forget it, no money coming in. Common sense always speaks too late. Common sense is the guy who tells you you ought to have had your brakes relined last week before you smashed a front end this week. Common sense is the Monday morning quarterback who could have won the ball game if he had been on the team. But he never is. He's high up in the stands with a flask on his hip. Common sense is the little man in a gray suit who never makes a mistake in addition. But it's always somebody else's money he's adding up.

At the turn-off I dipped down into the canyon and ended up at the Rancho Descansado. Jack and Lucille were in their usual positions. I dropped my suitcase and leaned on the desk.

"Did I leave the right change?"

"Yes, thanks," Jack said. "And now you want the room back, I suppose."

"If possible."

"Why didn't you tell us you were a detective?"

"Now, what a question." I grinned at him. "Does a detective ever tell anyone he's a detective? You watch TV, don't you?"

"When I get a chance. Not too often here."

"You can always tell a detective on TV. He never takes his hat off. What do you know about Larry Mitchell?"

"Nothing," Jack said stiffly. "He's a friend of Brandon's. Mr. Brandon owns this place."

Lucille said brightly: "Did you find Joe Harms all right?"

"Yes, thanks."

"And did you—?"

"Uh-huh."

"Button the lip, kid," Jack said tersely. He winked at me and pushed the key across the counter. "Lucille has a dull life, Mr. Marlowe. She's stuck here with me and a PBX. And an itty-bitty diamond ring—so small I was ashamed to give it to her. But what can a man do? If he loves a girl, he'd like it to show on her finger."

Lucille held her left hand up and moved it around to get a flash from the little stone. "I hate it," she said. "I hate it like I hate the sunshine and the summer and the bright stars and the full moon. That's how I hate it."

I picked up the key and my suitcase and left them. A little more of that and I'd be falling in love with myself. I might even give myself a small unpretentious diamond ring.

15

THE HOUSE PHONE at the Casa del Poniente got no reply from Room 1224. I walked over to the desk. A stiff-looking clerk was sorting letters. They are always sorting letters.

"Miss Mayfield is registered here, isn't she?" I asked.

He put a letter in a box before he answered me. "Yes, sir. What name shall I say?"

"I know her room number. She doesn't answer. Have you seen her today?"

He gave me a little more of his attention, but I didn't really send him. "I don't think so." He glanced over his shoulder. "Her key is out. Would you care to leave a message?"

"I'm a little worried. She wasn't well last night. She could be up there sick, not able to answer the phone. I'm a friend of hers. Marlowe's the name."

He looked me over. His eyes were wise eyes. He went behind a screen in the direction of the cashier's office and spoke to somebody. He came back in a short time. He was smiling.

"I don't think Miss Mayfield is ill, Mr. Marlowe. She ordered quite a substantial breakfast in her room. And lunch. She has had several telephone calls."

"Thanks a lot," I said. "I'll leave a message. Just my name and that I'll call back later."

"She might be out in the grounds or down on the beach," he said. "We have a warm beach, well sheltered by a breakwater." He glanced at the clock behind him. "If she is, she won't be there much longer. It's getting cool by now."

"Thanks. I'll be back."

The main part of the lobby was up three steps and through an arch. There were people in it just sitting, the dedicated hotel lounge sitters, usually elderly, usually rich, usually doing nothing but watching with hungry eyes. They spend their lives that way. Two old ladies with severe faces and purplish permanents were struggling with an enormous jigsaw puzzle set out on a specially built king-size card table. Farther along there was a canasta game going—two women, two men. One of the women had enough ice on her to cool the Mojave Desert and enough make-up to paint a steam yacht. Both women had cigarettes in long holders. The men with them looked gray and tired, probably from signing checks. Farther along, still sitting where they could look out through the glass, a young couple were holding hands. The girl had a diamond and emerald sparkler and a wedding ring which she kept touching with her fingertips. She looked a little dazed.

I went out through the bar and poked around in the gardens. I went along the path that threaded the cliff top and had no trouble picking out the spot I had looked down on the night before from Betty Mayfield's balcony. I could pick it out because of the sharp angle.

The bathing beach and small curved breakwater were a hundred yards along. Steps led down to it from the cliff. People were lying around on the sand. Some in swim suits or trunks, some just sitting there on rugs. Kids ran around screaming. Betty Mayfield was not on the beach.

I went back into the hotel and sat in the lounge.

I sat and smoked. I went to the newsstand and bought an evening paper and looked through it and threw it away. I strolled by the desk. My note was still in Box 1224. I went to the house phones and called Mr. Mitchell. No answer. I'm sorry. Mr. Mitchell does not answer his telephone.

A woman's voice spoke behind me "The clerk said you wanted to see me. Mr. Marlowe—" she said. "Are you Mr. Marlowe?"

She looked as fresh as a morning rose. She was wearing dark green slacks and saddle shoes and a green windbreaker over a white shirt with a loose Paisley scarf around that. A bandeau on her hair made a nice wind-blown effect.

The bell captain was hanging out his ear six feet away. I said: "Miss Mayfield?"

"I'm Miss Mayfield."

"I have the car outside. Do you have time to look at the property?"

She looked at her wrist watch. "Ye-es, I guess so," she said. "I ought to change pretty soon, but—oh, all right."

"This way, Miss Mayfield."

She fell in beside me. We walked across the lobby. I was getting to feel quite at home there. Betty Mayfield glanced viciously at the two jigsaw puzzlers.

"I hate hotels," she said. "Come back here in fifteen years and you would find the same people sitting in the same chairs."

"Yes, Miss Mayfield. Do you know anybody named Clyde Ummey?"

She shook her head. "Should I?"

"Helen Vermilyea? Ross Goble?"

She shook her head again.

"Want a drink?"

"Not now, thanks."

We came out of the bar and went along the walk and I held the door of the Olds for her. I backed out of the slot and pointed it straight up Grand Street towards the hills. She slipped dark glasses with spangled rims on her nose. "I found the traveler's checks," she said. "You're a queer sort of detective."

I reached in my pocket and held out her bottle of

sleeping pills. "I was a little scared last night," I said. "I counted these but I didn't know how many had been there to start with. You said you took two. I couldn't be sure you wouldn't rouse up enough to gulp a handful."

She took the bottle and stuffed it into her windbreaker. "I had quite a few drinks. Alcohol and barbiturates make a bad combination. I sort of passed out. It was nothing else."

"I wasn't sure. It takes a minimum of thirty-five grains of that stuff to kill. Even then it takes several hours. I was in a tough spot. Your pulse and breathing seemed all right but maybe they wouldn't be later on. If I called a doctor, I might have to do a lot of talking. If you had taken an overdose, the homicide boys would be told, even if you snapped out of it. They investigate all suicide attempts. But if I guessed wrong, you wouldn't be riding with me today. And where would I be then?"

"It's a thought," she said. "I can't say I'm going to worry about it terribly. Who are these people you mentioned?"

"Clyde Umney's the lawyer who hired me to follow you—on instructions from a firm of attorneys in Washington, D.C. Helen Vermilyea is his secretary. Ross Goble is a Kansas City private eye who says he is trying to find Mitchell." I described him to her.

Her face turned stony. "Mitchell? Why should he be interested in Larry?"

I stopped at the corner of Fourth and Grand for an old coot in a motorized wheel chair to make a left turn at four miles an hour. Esmeralda is full of the damn things.

"Why should he be looking for Larry Mitchell?" she asked bitterly. "Can't anybody leave anybody else alone?"

"Don't tell me anything," I said. "Just keep on asking me questions to which I don't know the answers. It's good for my inferiority complex. I told you I had no more job. So why am I here? That's easy. I'm groping for that five grand in traveler's checks again."

"Turn left at the next corner," she said, "and we can go up into the hills. There's a wonderful view from up there. And a lot of very fancy homes."

"The hell with them," I said.

"It's also very quiet up there." She picked a cigarette out of the pack clipped to the dash and lit it.

"That's two in two days," I said. "You're hitting them hard. I counted your cigarettes last night too. And your matches. I went through your bag. I'm kind of snoopy when I get roped in on a phony like that one. Especially when the client passes out and leaves me holding the baby."

She turned her head to stare at me. "It must have been the dope and the liquor," she said. "I must have been a little off base."

"Over at the Rancho Descansado you were in great shape. You were hard as nails. We were going to take off for Rio and live in luxury. Apparently also in sin. All I had to do was get rid of the body. What a letdown! No body."

She was still staring at me, but I had to watch my driving. I made a boulevard stop and a left turn. I went along another dead-end street with old streetcar tracks still in the paving.

"Turn left up the hill at that sign. That's the high school down there."

"Who fired the gun and what at?"

She pressed her temples with the heels of her hands. "I guess *I* must have. I must have been crazy. Where is it?"

"The gun? It's safe. Just in case your dream came true, I might have to produce it."

We were climbing now. I set the pointer to hold the Olds in third. She watched that with interest. She looked around her at the pale leather seats and the gadgets.

"How can you afford an expensive car like this? You don't make a lot of money, do you?"

"They're all expensive nowadays, even the cheap

ones. Fellow might as well have one that can travel. I read somewhere that a dick should always have a plain dark inconspicuous car that nobody would notice. The guy had never been to L.A. In L.A. to be conspicuous you would have to drive a flesh-pink Mercedes-Benz with a sun porch on the roof and three pretty girls sunbathing."

She giggled.

"Also," I labored the subject, "it's good advertising. Maybe I dreamed I was going to Rio. I could sell it there for more than it set me back new. On a freighter it wouldn't cost too much to ferry."

She sighed. "Oh, stop teasing me about that. I don't feel funny today."

"Seen your boy friend around?"

She sat very still. "Larry?"

"You got others?"

"Well—you might have meant Clark Brandon, althought I hardly know him. Larry was pretty drunk last night. No—I haven't seen him. Perhaps he's sleeping it off."

"Doesn't answer his phone."

The road forked. One white line curved to the left. I kept straight on, for no particular reason. We passed some old Spanish houses built high on the slope and some very modern houses built downhill on the other side. The road passed these and made a wide turn to the right. The paving here looked new. The road ran out to a point of land and a turning circle. There were two big houses facing each other across the turning circle. They were loaded with glass brick and their seaward windows were green glass. The view was magnificent. I looked at it for all of three seconds. I stopped against the end curb and cut the motor and sat. We were about a thousand feet up and the whole town was spread out in front of us like a 45 degree air photo.

"He might be sick," I said. "He might have gone out. He might even be dead."

"I told you—" She began to shake. I took the stub

of the cigarette away from her and put it in the ash tray. I ran the car windows up and put an arm around her shoulders and pulled her head down on my shoulder. She was limp, unresisting; but she still shook.

"You're a comfortable man," she said. "But don't rush me."

"There's a pint in the glove compartment. Want a snort?"

"Yes."

I got it out and managed to pull the metal strip loose with one hand and my teeth. I held the bottle between my knees and got the cap off. I held it to her lips. She sucked some in and shuddered. I recapped the pint and put it away.

"I hate drinking from the bottle," she said.

"Yeah. Unrefined. I'm not making love to you, Betty. I'm worried. Anything you want done?"

She was silent for a moment. Then her voice was steady, saying: "Such as what? You can have those checks back. They were yours. I gave them to you."

"Nobody gives anybody five grand like that. It makes no sense. That's why I came back down from L.A. I drove up there early this morning. Nobody goes all gooey over a character like me and talks about having half a million dollars and offers me a trip to Rio and a nice home complete with all the luxuries. Nobody drunk or sober does that because she dreamed a dead man was lying out on her balcony and would I please hurry around and throw him off into the ocean. Just what did you expect me to do when I got there— hold your hand while you dreamed?"

She pulled away and leaned in the far corner of the car. "All right, I'm a liar. I've always been a liar."

I glanced at the rear view mirror. Some kind of small dark car had turned into the road behind and stopped. I couldn't see who or what was in it. Then it swung hard right against the curbing and backed and made off the way it had come. Some fellow took the wrong road and saw it was a dead end.

"While I was on the way up those damn fire stairs,"

I went on, "you swallowed your pills and then faked being awfully terribly sleepy and then after a while you actually did go to sleep—I think. Okay. I went out on the balcony. No stiff. No blood. If there had been, I might have managed to get him over the top of the wall. Hard work, but not impossible, if you know how to lift. But six trained elephants couldn't have thrown him far enough to land in the ocean. It's thirty-five feet to the fence and you'd have to throw him so far out that he would clear the fence. I figure an object as heavy as a man's body would have to be thrown a good fifty feet outward to clear the fence."

"I told you I was a liar."

"But you didn't tell me why. Let's be serious. Suppose a man had been dead on your balcony. What would you expect me to do about it? Carry him down the fire stairs and get him into the car I had and drive off into the woods somewhere and bury him? You do have to take people into your confidence once in a while when bodies are lying around."

"You took my money," she said tonelessly. "You played up to me."

"That way I might find out who was crazy."

"You found out. You should be satisfied."

"I found out nothing—not even who you are."

She got angry. "I told you I was out of my mind," she said in a rushing voice. "Worry, fear, liquor, pills—why can't you leave me alone? I told you I'd give you back that money. What more do you want?"

"What do I do for it?"

"Just take it." She was snapping at me now. "That's all. Take it and go away. Far, far away."

"I think you need a good lawyer."

"That's a contradiction in terms," she sneered. "If he was good, he wouldn't be a lawyer."

"Yeah. So you've had some painful experience along those lines. I'll find out in time, either from you or some other way. But I'm still being serious. You're in trouble. Apart from what happened to Mitchell, if anything, you're in enough trouble to justify hiring yourself a lawyer. You changed your name. So you had reasons. Mitchell was putting the bite on you. So *he* had reasons. A firm of Washington attorneys is looking for you. So *they* have reasons. And their client has reasons to have them looking for you."

I stopped and looked at her as well as I could see her in the freshly darkening evening. Down below, the ocean was getting a lapis lazuli blue that somehow failed to remind me of Miss Vermilyea's eyes. A flock of gulls went south in a fairly compact mass but it wasn't the kind of tight formation North Island is used to. The evening plane from L.A. came down the coast with its port and starboard lights showing, and then the winking light below the fuselage went on and it swung out to sea for a long lazy turn into Lindbergh Field.

"So you're just a shill for a crooked lawyer," she said nastily, and grabbed for another of my cigarettes.

"I don't think he's very crooked. He just tries too hard. But that's not the point. You can lose a few bucks to him without screaming. The point is something called privilege. A licensed investigator doesn't have it. A lawyer does, provided his concern is with the interests of a client who has retained him. If the lawyer hires an investigator to work in those interests, then the investigator has privilege. That's the only way he can get it."

"You know what you can do with your privilege," she said. "Especially as it was a lawyer that hired you to spy on me."

I took the cigarette away from her and puffed on it a couple of times and handed it back.

"It's all right, Betty. I'm no use to you. Forget I tried to be."

"Nice words, but only because you think I'll pay you more to be of use to me. You're just another of them. I don't want your damn cigarette either." She threw it out of the window. "Take me back to the hotel."

I got out of the car and stamped on the cigarette. "You don't do that in the California hills," I told her. "Not even out of season." I got back into the car and turned the key and pushed the starter button. I backed away and made the turn and drove back up the curve to where the road divided. On the upper level where the solid white line curved away a small car was parked. The car was lightless. It could have been empty.

I swung the Olds hard the opposite way from the way I had come, and flicked my headlights on with the high beam. They swept the cars as I turned. A hat went down over a face, but not quick enough to hide the glasses, the fat broad face, the outjutting ears of Mr. Ross Goble of Kansas City.

The lights went on past and I drove down a long hill with lazy curves. I didn't know where it went except that all roads around there led to the ocean sooner or later. At the bottom there was a T-intersection. I swung to the right and after a few blocks of narrow street I hit the boulevard and made another right turn. I was now driving back towards the main part of Esmeralda.

She didn't speak again until I got to the hotel. She jumped out quickly when I stopped.

"If you'll wait here, I'll get the money."

"We were tailed," I said.

"What—?" She stopped dead, with her head half turned.

"Small car. You didn't notice him unless you saw my lights brush him as I made the turn at the top of the hill."

"Who was it?" Her voice was tense.

"How would I know? He must have picked us up here, therefore he'll come back here. Could he be a cop?"

She looked back at me, motionless, frozen. She took a slow step, and then she rushed at me as if she was going to claw my face. She grabbed me by the arms and tried to shake me. Her breath came whistling.

"Get me out of here. Get me out of here, for the love of Christ. Anywhere. Hide me. Get me a little peace. Somewhere where I can't be followed, hounded, threatened. He swore he would do it to me. He'd follow me to the ends of the earth, to the remotest island of the Pacific—"

"To the crest of the highest mountain, to the heart of the loneliest desert," I said. "Somebody's been reading a rather old-fashioned book."

She dropped her arms and let them hang limp at her sides.

"You've got as much sympathy as a loan shark."

"I'll take you nowhere," I said. "Whatever it is that's eating you, you're going to stay put and take it."

I turned and got into the car. When I looked back, she was already halfway to the bar entrance, walking with quick strides.

16

IF I HAD any sense, I would pick up my suitcase and
go back home and forget all about her. By the time she
made up her mind which part she was playing in which
act of which play, it would probably be too late for me
to do anything about it except maybe get pinched for
loitering in the post office.

I waited and smoked a cigarette. Goble and his dirty
little jalopy ought to show up and slip into a parking
slot almost any moment. He couldn't have picked us
up anywhere else, and since he knew that much he
couldn't have followed us for any reason except to find
out where we went.

He didn't show. I finished the cigarette, dropped it
overboard, and backed out. As I turned out of the
driveway towards the town, I saw his car on the other
side of the street, parked left-hand to the curb. I kept
going, turned right at the boulevard and took it easy so
he wouldn't blow a gasket trying to keep up. There
was a restaurant about a mile along called The Epi-
cure. It had a low roof, and a red brick wall to shield it
from the street and it had a bar. The entrance was at
the side. I parked and went in. It wasn't doing any
business yet. The barkeep was chatting with the captain and the captain didn't even wear a dinner jacket.
He had one of those high desks where they keep the

reservation book. The book was open and had a list of names in it for later in the evening. But it was early now. I could have a table.

The dining room was dim, candlelit, divided by a low wall into two halves. It would have looked crowded with thirty people in it. The captain shoved me in a corner and lit my candle for me. I said I would have a double Gibson. A waiter came up and started to remove the place setting on the far side of the table. I told him to leave it, a friend might join me. I studied the menu, which was almost as large as the dining room. I could have used a flashlight to read it, if I had been curious. This was about the dimmest joint I was ever in. You could be sitting at the next table from your mother and not recognize her.

The Gibson arrived. I could make out the shape of the glass and there seemed to be something in it. I tasted it and it wasn't too bad. At that moment Goble slid into the chair across from me. In so far as I could see him at all, he looked about the same as he had looked the day before. I went on peering at the menu. They ought to have printed it in braille.

Goble reached across for my glass of ice water and drank. "How you making out with the girl?" he asked casually.

"Not getting anywhere. Why?"

"Whatcha go up on the hill for?"

"I thought maybe we could neck. She wasn't in the mood. What's your interest? I thought you were looking for some guy named Mitchell."

"Very funny indeed. Some guy named Mitchell. Never heard of him, I believe you said."

"I've heard of him since. I've seen him. He was drunk. Very drunk. He damn near got himself thrown out of a place."

"Very funny," Goble said, sneering. "And how did you know his name?"

"On account of somebody called him by it. That would be *too* funny, wouldn't it?"

He sneered. "I told you to stay out of my way. I know who you are now. I looked you up."

I lit a cigarette and blew smoke in his face. "Go fry a stale egg."

"Tough, huh," he sneered. "I've pulled the arms and legs off bigger guys than you."

"Name two of them."

He leaned across the table, but the waiter came up.

"I'll have bourbon and plain water," Goble told him. "Bonded stuff. None of that bar whiskey for me. And don't try to fool me. I'll know. And bottled water. The city water here is terrible."

The waiter just looked at him.

"I'll have another of these," I said, pushing my glass.

"What's good tonight?" Goble wanted to know. "I never bother with these billboards." He flicked a disdainful finger at the menu.

"The *plat du jour* is meat loaf," the waiter said nastily.

"Hash with a starched collar," Goble said. "Make it meat loaf."

The waiter looked at me. I said the meat loaf was all right with me. The waiter went away. Goble leaned across the table again, after first taking a quick look behind him and on both sides.

"You're out of luck, friend," he said cheerfully. "You didn't get away with it."

"Too bad," I said. "Get away with what?"

"You're bad out of luck, friend. Very bad. The tide was wrong or something. Abalone fisher—one of those guys with frog feet and rubber masks—stuck under a rock."

"The abalone fisher stuck under a rock?" A cold prickly feeling crawled down my back. When the waiter came with the drinks, I had to fight myself not to grab for mine.

"Very funny, friend."

"Say that again and I'll smash your goddam glasses for you," I snarled.

He picked up his drink and sipped it, tasted it, thought about it, nodded his head.

"I came out here to make money," he mused. "I didn't nowise come out to make trouble. Man can't make money making trouble. Man can make money keeping his nose clean. Get me?"

"Probably a new experience for you," I said. "Both ways. What was that about an abalone fisher?" I kept my voice controlled, but it was an effort.

He leaned back. My eyes were getting used to the dimness now. I could see that his fat face was amused.

"Just kidding," he said. "I don't know any abalone fishers. Only last night I learned how to pronounce the word. Still don't know what the stuff is. But things are kind of funny at that. I can't find Mitchell."

"He lives at the hotel." I took some more of my drink, not too much. This was no time to dive into it.

"I know he lives at the hotel, friend. What I don't know is where he is at right now. He ain't in his room. The hotel people ain't seen him around. I thought maybe you and the girl had some ideas about it."

"The girl is screwy," I said. "Leave her out of it. And in Esmeralda they don't say 'ain't seen.' That Kansas City dialect is an offense against public morals here."

"Shove it, Mac. When I want to get told how to talk English I won't go to no beat-up California peeper." He turned his head and yelled: "Waiter!"

Several faces looked at him with distaste. The waiter showed up after a while and stood there with the same expression as the customers.

"Hit me again," Goble said, snapped a finger at his glass.

"It is not necessary to yell at me," the waiter said. He took the glass away.

"When I want service," Goble yelped at his back, "service is what I want."

"I hope you like the taste of wood alcohol," I told Goble.

"Me and you could get along," Goble said indifferently, "if you had any brains."

"And if you had any manners and were six inches taller and had a different face and another name and didn't act as if you thought you could lick your weight in frog spawn."

"Cut the doodads and get back to Mitchell," he said briskly. "And to the dish you was trying to fumble up the hill."

"Mitchell is a man she met on a train. He had the same effect on her that you have on me. He created in her a burning desire to travel in the opposite direction."

It was a waste of time. The guy was as invulnerable as my great-great-grandfather.

"So," he sneered, "Mitchell to her is just a guy she met on a train and didn't like when she got to know him. So she ditched him for you? Convenient you happened to be around."

The waiter came with the food. He set it out with a flourish. Vegetables, salad, hot rolls in a napkin.

"Coffee?"

I said I'd rather have mine later. Goble said yes and wanted to know where his drink was. The waiter said it was on the way—by slow freight, his tone suggested. Goble tasted his meat loaf and looked surprised. "Hell, it's good," he said. "What with so few customers I thought the place was a bust."

"Look at your watch," I said. "Things don't get moving until much later. It's that kind of town. Also, it's out of season."

"Much later is right," he said, munching. "An awful lot later. Two, three in the A.M. sometimes. People go calling on their friends. You back at the Rancho, friend?"

I looked at him without saying anything.

"Do I have to draw you a picture, friend? I work long hours when I'm on a job."

I didn't say anything.

He wiped his mouth. "You kind of stiffened up

when I said that about the guy stuck under a rock. Or could I be wrong?"

I didn't answer him.

"Okay, clam up," Goble sneered. "I thought maybe we could do a little business together. You got the physique and you take a good punch. But you don't know nothing about nothing. You don't have what it takes in my business. Where I come from you got to have brains to get by. Out here you just got to get sunburned and forget to button your collar."

"Make me a proposition," I said between my teeth.

He was a rapid eater even when he talked too much. He pushed his plate away from him, drank some of his coffee and got a toothpick out of his vest.

"This is a rich town, friend," he said slowly. "I've studied it. I've boned up on it. I've talked to guys about it. They tell me it's one of the few spots left in our fair green country where the dough ain't quite enough. In Esmeralda you got to belong, or you're nothing. If you want to belong and get asked around and get friendly with the right people you got to have class. There's a guy here made five million fish in the rackets back in Kansas City. He brought up property, subdivided, built houses, built some of the best properties in town. But he didn't belong to the Beach Club because he didn't get asked. So he bought it. They know who he is, they touch him big when they got a fund-raising drive, he gets service, he pays his bills, he's a good solid citizen. He throws big parties but the guests come from out of town unless they're moochers, no-goods, the usual trash you always find hopping about where there's money. But the class people of the town? He's just a nigger to them."

It was a long speech and while he made it he glanced at me casually from time to time, glanced around the room, leaned back comfortably in his chair and picked his teeth.

"He must be breaking his heart," I said. "How did they find out where his dough came from?"

Goble leaned across the small table. "A big shot

from the Treasury Department comes here for a vacation every spring. Happened to see Mr. Money and know all about him. He spread the word. You think it's not breaking his heart? You don't know these hoods that have made theirs and gone respectable. He's bleeding to death inside, friend. He's found something he can't buy with folding money and it's eating him to a shell."

"How did you find out all this?"

"I'm smart. I get around. I find things out."

"All except one," I said.

"Just what's that?"

"You wouldn't know if I told you."

The waiter came up with Goble's delayed drink and took dishes away. He offered the menu.

"I never eat dessert," Goble said. "Scram."

The waiter looked at the toothpick. He reached over and deftly flicked it out from between Goble's fingers. "There's a Men's Room here, chum," he said. He dropped the toothpick into the ash tray and removed the ash tray.

"See what I mean?" Goble said to me. "Class."

I told the waiter I would have a chocolate sundae and some coffee. "And give this gentleman the check," I added.

"A pleasure," the waiter said. Goble looked disgusted. The waiter drifted. I leaned across the table and spoke softly.

"You're the biggest liar I've met in two days. And I've met a few beauties. I don't think you have any interest in Mitchell. I don't think you ever saw or heard of him until yesterday when you got the idea of using him as a cover story. You were sent here to watch a girl and I know who sent you—not who hired you, but who had it done. I know why she is being watched and I know how to fix it so that she won't be watched. If you've got any high cards, you'd better play them right away quick. Tomorrow could be too late."

He pushed his chair back and stood up. He dropped

a folded and crimped bill on the table. He looked me over coolly.

"Big mouth, small brain," he said. "Save it for Thursday when they set the trash cans out. You don't know from nothing, friend. My guess is you never will."

He walked off with his head thrust forward belligerently.

I reached across for the folded and crimped bill Goble had dropped on the table. As I expected it was only a dollar. Any guy who would drive a jalopy that might be able to do forty-five miles an hour downhill would eat in joints where the eighty-five cent dinner was something for a wild Saturday night.

The waiter slid over and dumped the check on me. I paid up and left Goble's dollar in his plate.

"Thanks," the waiter said. "That guy's a real close friend of yours, huh?"

"The operative word is close," I said.

"The guy might be poor," the waiter said tolerantly. "One of the choice things about this town is that the people who work here can't afford to live here."

There were all of twenty people in the place when I left, and the voices were beginning to bounce down off the low ceiling.

17

THE RAMP down to the garage looked just the same as it had looked at four o'clock in the morning, but there was a swishing of water audible as I rounded the curve. The glassed-in cubicle office was empty. Somewhere somebody was washing a car, but it wouldn't be the attendant. I crossed to the door leading into the elevator lobby and held it open. The buzzer sounded behind me in the office. I let the door close and stood outside it waiting and a lean man in a long white coat came around the corner. He wore glasses, had a skin the color of cold oatmeal and hollow tired eyes. There was something Mongolian about his face, something south-of-the-border, something Indian, and something darker than that. His black hair was flat on a narrow skull.

"Your car, sir? What name, please?"

"Mr. Mitchell's car in? The two-tone Buick hardtop?"

He didn't answer right away. His eyes went to sleep. He had been asked that question before.

"Mr. Mitchell took his car out early this morning."

"How early?"

He reached for a pencil that was clipped to his pocket over the stitched-on scarlet script with the hotel name. He took the pencil out and looked at it.

"Just before seven o'clock. I went off at seven."

"You work a twelve-hour shift? It's only a little past seven now."

He put the pencil back in his pocket. "I work an eight-hour shift but we rotate."

"Oh. Last night you worked eleven to seven."

"That's right." He was looking past my shoulder at something far away. "I'm due off now."

I got out a pack of cigarettes and offered him one.

He shook his head.

"I'm only allowed to smoke in the office."

"Or in the back of a Packard sedan."

His right hand curled, as if around the haft of a knife.

"How's your supply? Needing anything?"

He stared.

"You should have said 'Supply of what?'" I told him.

He didn't answer.

"And I would have said I wasn't talking about tobacco," I went on cheerfully. "About something cured with honey."

Our eyes met and locked. Finally he said softly: "You a pusher?"

"You snapped out of it real nice, if you were in business at seven A.M. this morning. Looked to me as if you would be out of circulation for hours. You must have a clock in your head—like Eddie Arcaro."

"Eddie Arcaro," he repeated. "Oh yes, the jockey. Has a clock in his head, has he?"

"So they say."

"We might do business," he said remotely. "What's your price?"

The buzzer sounded in the office. I had heard the elevator in the shaft subconsciously. The door opened and the couple I had seen holding hands in the lobby came through. The girl had on an evening dress and the boy wore a tux. They stood side by side, looking like two kids who had been caught kissing. The attendant glanced at them and went off and a car started and came back. A nice new Chrysler convertible. The guy handed the girl in carefully, as if she was already pregnant. The attendant stood holding the door. The guy came around the car and thanked him and got in.

"Is it very far to The Glass Room?" he asked diffidently.

"No, sir." The attendant told them how to get there.

The guy smiled and thanked him and reached in his pocket and gave the attendant a dollar bill.

"You could have your car brought around to the entrance, Mr. Preston. All you have to do is call down."

"Oh thanks, but this is fine," the guy said hurriedly. He started carefully up the ramp. The Chrysler purred out of sight and was gone.

"Honeymooners," I said. "They're sweet. They just don't want to be stared at."

The attendant was standing in front of me again with the same flat look in his eyes.

"But there's nothing sweet about us," I added.

"If you're a cop, let's see the buzzer."

"You think I'm a cop?"

"You're some kind of nosy bastard." Nothing he said changed the tone of his voice at all. It was frozen in B Flat. Johnny One-Note.

"I'm all of that," I agreed. "I'm a private star. I followed somebody down here last night. You were in a Packard right over there"—I pointed—"and I went over and opened the door and sniffed the weed. I could have driven four Cadillacs out of here and you wouldn't have turned over in bed. But that's your business."

"The price today," he said. "I'm not arguing about last night."

"Mitchell left by himself?"

He nodded.

"No baggage?"

"Nine pieces. I helped him load it. He checked out. Satisfied?"

"You checked with the office?"

"He had his bill. All paid up and receipted."

"Sure. And with that amount of baggage a hop came with him naturally."

"The elevator kid. No hops on until seven-thirty. This was about one A.M."

"Which elevator kid?"

"A Mex kid we call Chico."

"You're not Mex?"

"I'm part Chinese, part Hawaiian, part Filipino, and part nigger. You'd hate to be me."

"Just one more question. How in hell do you get away with it? The muggles, I mean."

He looked around. "I only smoke when I feel extra special low. What the hell's it to you? What the hell's it to anybody? Maybe I get caught and lose a crummy job. Maybe I get tossed in a cell. Maybe I've been in one all my life, carry it round with me. Satisfied?" He was talking too much. People with unstable nerves are like that. One moment monosyllables, next moment a flood. The low tired monotone of his voice went on.

"I'm not sore at anybody. I live. I eat. Sometimes I sleep. Come around and see me some time. I live in a flea bag in an old frame cottage on Polton's Lane, which is really an alley. I live right behind the Esmeralda Hardware Company. The toilet's in a shed. I wash in the kitchen, at a tin sink. I sleep on a couch with broken springs. Everything there is twenty years old. This is a rich man's town. Come and see me. I live on a rich man's property."

"There's a piece missing from your story about Mitchell," I said.

"Which one?"

"The truth."

"I'll look under the couch for it. It might be a little dusty."

There was the rough noise of a car entering the ramp from above. He turned away and I went through the door and rang for the elevator. He was a queer duck, the attendant, very queer. Kind of interesting, though. And kind of sad, too. One of the sad, one of the lost.

The elevator was a long time coming and before it came I had company waiting for it. Six feet three inches of handsome, healthy male named Clark Brandon. He was wearing a leather windbreaker and a heavy roll-collar blue sweater under it, a pair of beat-up Bedford cord breeches, and the kind of high laced boots that field engineers and surveyors wear in rough country. He looked like the boss of a drilling crew. In an hour from now, I had no doubt he would be at The Glass Room in a dinner suit and he would look like the boss of that too, and perhaps he was. Plenty of money, plenty of health and plenty of time to get the best out of both, and wherever he went he would be the owner.

He glanced at me and waited for me to get into the elevator when it came. The elevator kid saluted him respectfully. He nodded. We both got off at the lobby. Brandon crossed to the desk and got a big smile from the clerk—a new one I hadn't seen before—and the clerk handed him a fistful of letters. Brandon leaned against the end of the counter and tore the envelopes open one by one and dropped them into a wastebasket beside where he was standing. Most of the letters went the same way. There was a rack of travel folders there. I picked one off and lit a cigarette and studied the folder.

Brandon had one letter that interested him. He read it several times. I could see that it was short and hand-written on the hotel stationery, but without looking over his shoulder that was all I could see. He stood holding the letter. Then he reached down into the basket and came up with the envelope. He studied that. He put the letter in his pocket and moved along the desk. He handed the clerk the envelope.

"This was handed in. Did you happen to see who left it? I don't seem to know the party."

The clerk looked at the envelope and nodded. "Yes, Mr. Brandon, a man left it just after I came on. He was a middle-aged fat man with glasses. Gray suit and topcoat and gray felt hat. Not a local type. A little shabby. A nobody."

"Did he ask for me?"

"No, sir. Just asked me to put the note in your box. Anything wrong, Mr. Brandon?"

"Look like a goof?"

The clerk shook his head. "He just looked what I said. Like a nobody."

Brandon chuckled. "He wants to make me a Mormon bishop for fifty dollars. Some kind of nut, obviously." He picked the envelope up off the counter and put it in his pocket. He started to turn away, then said: "Seen Larry Mitchell around?"

"Not since I've been on, Mr. Brandon. But that's only a couple of hours."

"Thanks."

Brandon walked across to the elevator and got in. It was a different elevator. The operator grinned all over his face and said something to Brandon. Brandon didn't answer him or look at him. The kid looked hurt as he whooshed the doors shut. Brandon was scowling. He was less handsome when he scowled.

I put the travel folder back in the rack and moved over to the desk. The clerk looked at me without interest. His glance said I was not registered there. "Yes, sir?"

He was a gray-haired man who carried himself well.

"I was just going to ask for Mr. Mitchell, but I heard what you said."

"The house phones are over there." He pointed with his chin. "The operator will connect you."

"I doubt it."

"Meaning what?"

I pulled my jacket open to get at my letter case. I could see the clerk's eyes freeze on the rounded butt of the gun under my arm. I got the letter case out and pulled a card.

"Would it be convenient for me to see your house man? If you have one."

He took the card and read it. He looked up. "Have a seat in the main lobby, Mr. Marlowe."

"Thank you."

He was on the phone before I had done a complete

turn away from the desk. I went through the arch and sat against the wall where I could see the desk. I didn't have very long to wait.

The man had a hard straight back and a hard straight face, with the kind of skin that never tans but only reddens and pales out again. His hair was almost a pompadour and mostly reddish blond. He stood in the archway and let his eyes take in the lobby slowly. He didn't look at me any longer than at anybody else. Then he came over and sat down in the next chair to me. He wore a brown suit and a brown and yellow bow tie. His clothes fitted him nicely. There were fine blond hairs on his cheeks high up. There was a grace note of gray in his hair.

"My name's Javonen," he said without looking at me. "I know yours. Got your card in my pocket. What's your trouble?"

"Man named Mitchell. I'm looking for him. Larry Mitchell."

"You're looking for him why?"

"Business. Any reason why I shouldn't look for him?"

"No reason at all. He's out of town. Left early this morning."

"So I heard. It puzzled me some. He only got home yesterday. On the Super Chief. In L.A. he picked up his car and drove down. Also, he was broke. Had to make a touch for dinner money. He ate dinner at The Glass Room with a girl. He was pretty drunk—or pretended to be. It got him out of paying the check."

"He can sign his checks here," Javonen said indifferently. His eyes kept flicking around the lobby as if he expected to see one of the canasta players yank a gun and shoot his partner or one of the old ladies at the big jigsaw puzzle start pulling hair. He had two expressions—hard and harder. "Mr. Mitchell is well known in Esmeralda."

"Well, but not favorably," I said.

He turned his head and gave me a bleak stare. "I'm an assistant manager here, Mr. Marlowe. I double as security officer. I can't discuss the reputation of a guest of the hotel with you."

"You don't have to. I know it. From various sources. I've observed him in action. Last night he put the bite on somebody and got enough to blow town. Taking his baggage with him, is my information."

"Who gave this information to you?" He looked tough asking that.

I tried to look tough not answering it. "On top of that I'll give you three guesses," I said. "One, his bed wasn't slept in last night. Two, it was reported to the office sometime today that his room had been cleaned out. Three, somebody on your night staff won't show for work tonight. Mitchell couldn't get all his stuff out without help."

Javonen looked at me, then prowled the lobby again with his eyes. "Got something that proves you are what the card reads? Anyone can have a card printed."

I got my wallet out and slipped a small photostat of my license from it and passed it over. He glanced at it and handed it back. I put it away.

"We have our own organization to take care of skipouts," he said. "They happen—in any hotel. We don't need your help. And we don't like guns in the lobby. The clerk saw yours. Somebody else could see it. We had a stickup attempted here nine months ago. One of the heist guys got dead. I shot him."

"I read about it in the paper," I said. "It scared me for days and days."

"You read some of it. We lost four or five thousand dollars worth of business the week following. People checked out by the dozen. You get my point?"

"I let the clerk see my gunbutt on purpose. I've been asking for Mitchell all day and all I got was the runaround. If the man checked out, why not say so? Nobody had to tell me he had jumped his bill."

"Nobody said he jumped his bill. His bill, Mr. Marlowe, was paid in full. So where does that leave you?"

"Wondering why it was a secret he had checked out."

He looked contemptuous. "Nobody said that either. You don't listen good. I said he was out of town on a trip. I said his bill was paid in full. I didn't say how much baggage he took. I didn't say he had given up his room. I didn't say that what he took was all he had ... Just what are you trying to make out of all this?"

"Who paid his bill?"

His face got a little red. "Look, buster, I told you *he* paid it. In person, last night, in full and a week in advance as well. I've been pretty patient with you. Now you tell me something. What's your angle?"

"I don't have one. You've talked me out of it. I wonder why he paid a week in advance."

Javonen smiled—very slightly. Call it a down payment on a smile. "Look, Marlowe, I put in five years in Military Intelligence. I can size up a man—like for instance the guy we're talking about. He pays in advance because we feel happier that way. It has a stabilizing influence."

"He ever pay in advance before?"

"God damn it. . . !"

"Watch yourself," I cut in. "The elderly gent with the walking stick is interested in your reactions."

He looked halfway across the lobby to where a thin, old, bloodless man sat in a very low round-backed padded chair with his chin on gloved hands and the gloved hands on the crook of a stick. He stared unblinkingly in our direction.

"Oh, him," Javonen said. "He can't even see this far. He's eighty years old."

He stood up and faced me. "Okay, you're clammed," he said quietly. "You're a private op, you've got a client and instructions. I'm only interested in protecting the hotel. Leave the gun home next time. If you have questions, come to me. Don't question the help. It gets told around and we don't like it. You wouldn't find the local cops friendly if I suggested you were being troublesome."

"Can I buy a drink in the bar before I go?"

"Keep your jacket buttoned."

"Five years in Military Intelligence is a lot of experience," I said looking up at him admiringly.

"It ought to be enough." He nodded briefly and strolled away through the arch, back straight, shoulders back, chin in, a hard lean well set-up piece of man. A smooth operator. He had milked me dry—of everything that was printed on my business card.

Then I noticed that the old party in the low chair had lifted a gloved hand off the crook of his stick and was curving a finger at me. I pointed a finger at my chest and looked the question. He nodded, so over I went.

He was old, all right, but a long way from feeble and a long way from dim. His white hair was neatly parted, his nose was long and sharp and veined, his faded-out blue eyes were still keen, but the lids drooped wearily over them. One ear held the plastic button of a hearing aid, grayish pink like his ear. The suede gloves on his hands had the cuffs turned back. He wore gray spats over polished black shoes.

"Pull up a chair, young man." His voice was thin and dry and rustled like bamboo leaves.

I sat down beside him. He peered at me and his mouth smiled. "Our excellent Mr. Javonen spent five years in Military Intelligence, as no doubt he told you."

"Yes, sir. CIC, a branch of it."

"Military Intelligence is an expression which contains an interior fallacy. So you are curious about how Mr. Mitchell paid his bill?"

I stared at him. I looked at the hearing aid. He tapped his breast pocket. "I was deaf long before they invented these things. As the result of a hunter balking at a fence. It was my own fault. I lifted him too soon. I was still a young man. I couldn't see myself using an ear trumpet, so I learned to lip-read. It takes a certain amount of practice."

"What about Mitchell, sir?"

"We'll come to him. Don't be in a hurry." He looked up and nodded.

A voice said, "Good evening, Mr. Clarendon." A

bellhop went by on his way to the bar. Clarendon followed him with his eyes.

"Don't bother with that one," he said. "He's a pimp. I have spent many many years in lobbies, in lounges and bars, on porches, terraces and ornate gardens in hotels all over the world. I have outlived everyone in my family. I shall go on being useless and inquisitive until the day comes when the stretcher carries me off to some nice airy corner room in a hospital. The starched white dragons will minister to me. The bed will be wound up, wound down. Trays will come with that awful loveless hospital food. My pulse and temperature will be taken at frequent intervals and invariably when I am dropping off to sleep. I shall lie there and hear the rustle of the starched skirts, the slurring sound of the rubber shoe soles on the aseptic floor, and see the silent horror of the doctor's smile. After a while they will put the oxygen tent over me and draw the screens around the little white bed and I shall, without even knowing it, do the one thing in the world no man ever has to do twice."

He turned his head slowly and looked at me. "Obviously, I talk too much. Your name, sir?"

"Philip Marlowe."

"I am Henry Clarendon IV. I belong to what used to be called the upper classes. Groton, Harvard, Heidelberg, the Sorbonne. I even spent a year at Uppsala. I cannot clearly remember why. To fit me for a life of leisure, no doubt. So you are a private detective. I do eventually get around to speaking of something other than myself, you see."

"Yes, sir."

"You should have come to me for information. But of course you couldn't know that."

I shook my head. I lit a cigarette, first offering one to Mr. Henry Clarendon IV. He refused it with a vague nod.

"However, Mr. Marlowe, it is something you should have certainly learned. In every luxury hotel in the world there will be half a dozen elderly idlers of both sexes who sit around and stare like owls. They watch, they listen, they compare notes, they learn everything about everyone. They have nothing else to do, because hotel life is the most deadly of all forms of boredom. And no doubt I'm boring you equally."

"I'd rather hear about Mitchell, sir. Tonight at least, Mr. Clarendon."

"Of course. I'm egocentric, and absurd, and I prattle like a schoolgirl. You observe that handsome dark-haired woman over there playing canasta? The one with too much jewelry and the heavy gold trim on her glasses?"

He didn't point or even look. But I picked her out. She had an overblown style and she looked just a little hardboiled. She was the one with the ice, the paint.

"Her name is Margo West. She is seven times a divorcee. She has stacks of money and reasonably good looks, but she can't hold a man. She tries too hard. Yet she's not a fool. She would have an affair with a man like Mitchell, she would give him money and pay his bills, but she would never marry him. They had a fight last night. Nevertheless I believe she may have paid his bill. She often has before."

"I thought he got a check from his father in Toronto every month. Not enough to last him, huh?"

Henry Clarendon IV gave me a sardonic smile. "My dear fellow, Mitchell has no father in Toronto. He gets no monthly check. He lives on women. That is why he lives in a hotel like this. There is always some rich and lonely female in a luxury hotel. She may not be beautiful or very young, but she has other charms. In the dull season in Esmeralda, which is from the end of the race meet at Del Mar until about the middle of January, the pickings are very lean. Then Mitchell is apt to travel—Majorca or Switzerland if he can make it, to Florida or one of the Caribbean islands if he is not in rich funds. This year he had poor luck. I understand he only got as far as Washington."

He brushed a glance at me. I stayed deadpan polite,

just a nice youngish guy (by his standards) being polite to an old gentleman who liked to talk.

"Okay," I said. "She paid his hotel bill, maybe. But why a week in advance?"

He moved one gloved hand over the other. He tilted his stick and followed it with his body. He stared at the pattern in the carpet. Finally he clicked his teeth. He had solved the problem. He straightened up again.

"That would be severance pay," he said dryly. "The final and irrevocable end of the romance. Mrs. West, as the English say, had had it. Also, there was a new arrival in Mitchell's company yesterday, a girl with dark red hair. Chestnut red, not fire red or strawberry red. What I saw of their relationship seemed to me a little peculiar. They were both under some sort of strain."

"Would Mitchell blackmail a woman?"

He chuckled. "He would blackmail an infant in a cradle. A man who lives on women always blackmails them, although the word may not be used. He also steals from them when he can get his hands on any of their money. Mitchell forged two checks with Margo West's name. That ended the affair. No doubt she has the checks. But she won't do anything about it except keep them."

"Mr. Clarendon, with all due respect, how in hell would you know all these things?"

"She told me. She cried on my shoulder." He looked toward the handsome dark-haired woman. "She does not at the moment look as if I could be telling the truth. Nevertheless I am."

"And why are you telling it to me?"

His face moved into a rather ghastly grin. "I have no delicacy. I should like to marry Margo West myself. It would reverse the pattern. Very small things amuse a man of my age. A hummingbird, the extraordinary way a strellitzia bloom opens. Why at a certain point in its growth does the bud turn at right angles? Why does the bud split so gradually and why do the flowers emerge always in a certain exact order, so that the sharp unopened end of the bud looks like a bird's beak and the blue and orange petals make a bird of paradise? What strange deity made such a complicated world when presumably he could have made a simple one? Is he omnipotent? How could he be? There's so much suffering and almost always by the innocent. Why will a mother rabbit trapped in a burrow by a ferret put her babies behind her and allow her throat to be torn out? Why? In two weeks more she would not even recognize them. Do you believe in God, young man?"

It was a long way around, but it seemed I had to travel it. "If you mean an omniscient and omnipotent God who intended everything exactly the way it is, no."

"But you should, Mr. Marlowe. It is a great comfort. We all come to it in the end because we have to die and become dust. Perhaps for the individual that is all, perhaps not. There are grave difficulties about the afterlife. I don't think I should really enjoy a heaven in which I shared lodgings with a Congo pygmy or a Chinese coolie or a Levantine rug peddler or even a Hollywood producer. I'm a snob, I suppose, and the remark is in bad taste. Nor can I imagine a heaven presided over by a benevolent character in a long white beard locally known as God. These are foolish conceptions of very immature minds. But you may not question a man's religious beliefs however idiotic they may be. Of course I have no right to assume that I shall go to heaven. Sounds rather dull, as a matter of fact. On the other hand how can I imagine a hell in which a baby that died before baptism occupies the same degraded position as a hired killer or a Nazi death-camp commandant or a member of the Politburo? How strange it is that man's finest aspirations, dirty little animal that he is, his finest actions also, his great and unselfish heroism, his constant daily courage in a harsh world——how strange that these things should be so much finer than his fate on this earth. That has to be somehow made reasonable. Don't tell me that honor is merely a chemical reaction or that a man who deliberately gives his life for another is merely following a behavior pattern. Is God happy with the poisoned cat dying alone in convulsions behind the billboard? Is God happy that life is cruel and that only the fittest survive? The fittest for what? Oh no, far from it. If God were omnipotent and omniscient in any literal sense, he wouldn't have bothered to make the universe at all. There is no success where there is no possibility of failure, no art without the resistance of the medium. Is it blasphemy to suggest that God has his bad days when nothing goes right, and that God's days are very, very long?"

"You're a wise man, Mr. Clarendon. You said something about reversing the pattern."

He smiled faintly. "You thought I had lost the place in the overlong book of my words. No sir, I had not. A woman like Mrs. West almost always ends up marrying a series of pseudo-elegant fortune hunters, tango dancers with handsome sideburns, skiing instructors with beautiful blond muscles, faded French and Italian aristocrats, shoddy princelings from the Middle East, each worse than the one before. She might even in her extremity marry a man like Mitchell. If she married me, she would marry an old bore, but at least she would marry a gentleman."

"Yeah."

He chuckled. "The monosyllable indicates a surfeit of Henry Clarendon IV. I don't blame you. Very well, Mr. Marlowe, why are you interested in Mitchell? But I suppose you can't tell me."

"No sir, I can't. I'm interested in knowing why he left so soon after coming back, who paid his bill for him and why, if Mrs. West or, say, some well-heeled friend like Clark Brandon paid for him, it was necessary to pay a week in advance as well."

His thin worn eyebrows curved upwards. "Brandon could easily guarantee Mitchell's account by lifting the telephone. Mrs. West might prefer to give him the money and have him pay the bill himself. But a week in advance? Why would our Javonen tell you that? What does it suggest to you?"

"That there's something about Mitchell the hotel doesn't want known. Something that might cause the sort of publicity they hate."

"Such as?"

"Suicide and murder are the sort of things I mean. That's just by way of example. You've noticed how the name of a big hotel is hardly ever mentioned when one of the guests jumps out of a window? It's always a midtown or a downtown hotel or a well-known exclusive hotel—something like that. And it it's rather a high class place, you never see any cops in the lobby, no matter what happened upstairs."

His eyes went sideways and mine followed his. The canasta table was breaking up. The dolled-up and well-iced woman called Margo West strolled off towards the bar with one of the men, her cigarette holder sticking out like a bowsprit.

"So?"

"Well," I said, and I was working hard, "if Mitchell keeps his room on the records, whatever room he had—"

"Four-eighteen," Clarendon put in calmly. "On the ocean side. Fourteen dollars a day out of season, eighteen in season."

"Not exactly cheap for a guy on his uppers. But he still has it, let's say. So whatever happened, he's just away for a few days. Took his car out, put his luggage in around seven A.M. this morning. A damn funny time to leave when he was as drunk as a skunk late last night."

Clarendon leaned back and let his gloved hands hang limp. I could see that he was getting tired. "If it happened that way, wouldn't the hotel prefer to have you think he had left for good? Then you'd have to search for him somewhere else. That is, if you really are searching for him."

I met his pale stare. He grinned.

"You're not making very good sense to me, Mr. Marlowe. I talk and talk, but not merely to hear the sound of my voice. I don't hear it naturally in any case.

Talking gives me an opportunity to study people without seeming altogether rude. I have studied you. My intuition, if such be the correct word, tells me that your interest in Mitchell is rather tangential. Otherwise you would not be so open about it."

"Uh-huh. Could be," I said. It was a spot for a paragraph of lucid prose. Henry Clarendon IV would have obliged. I didn't have a damn thing more to say.

"Run along now," he said. "I'm tired. I'm going up to my room and lie down a little. A pleasure to have met you, Mr. Marlowe." He got slowly to his feet and steadied himself with the stick. It was an effort. I stood up beside him.

"I never shake hands," he said. "My hands are ugly and painful. I wear gloves for that reason. Good evening. If I don't see you again, good luck."

He went off, walking slowly and keeping his head erect. I could see that walking wasn't any fun for him. The two steps up from the main lobby to the arch were made one at a time, with a pause in between. His right foot always moved first. The cane bore down hard beside his left. He went out through the arch and I watched him move towards an elevator. I decided Mr. Henry Clarendon IV was a pretty smooth article.

I strolled along to the bar. Mrs. Margo West was sitting in the amber shadows with one of the canasta players. The waiter was just setting drinks before them. I didn't pay too much attention because farther along in a little booth against the wall was someone I knew better. And alone.

She had the same clothes on except that she had taken the bandeau off her hair and it hung loose around her face.

I sat down. The waiter came over and I ordered. He went away. The music from the invisible record player was low and ingratiating.

She smiled a little. "I'm sorry I lost my temper," she said. "I was very rude."

"Forget it. I had it coming."

"Were you looking for me in here?"

"Not especially."

"Were you—oh, I forgot." She reached for her bag and put it in her lap. She fumbled in it and then passed something rather small across the table, something not small enough for her hand to hide that it was a folder of traveler's checks. "I promised you these."

"No."

"Take them, you fool! I don't want the waiter to see."

I took the folder and slipped it into my pocket. I reached into my inside pocket and got out a small receipt book. I entered the counterfoil and then the body of the receipt. "Received from Miss Betty Mayfield, Hotel Casa del Poniente, Esmeralda, California, the sum of $5000 in American Express Company traveler's checks of $100 denomination, countersigned by the owner, and remaining her property subject to her demand at any time until a fee is arranged with, and an employment accepted by me, the undersigned."

I signed this rigmarole and held the book for her to see it.

"Read it and sign your name in the lower left-hand corner."

She took it and held it close to the light.

"You make me tired," she said. "Whatever are you trying to spring?"

"That I'm on the level and you think so."

She took the pen I held out and signed and gave the stuff back to me. I tore out the original and handed it to her. I put the book away.

The waiter came and put my drink down. He didn't wait to be paid. Betty shook her head at him. He went away.

"Why don't you ask me if I have found Larry?"

"All right. Have you found Larry, Mr. Marlowe?"

"No. He has skipped the hotel. He had a room on the fourth floor on the same side as your room. Must be fairly nearly under it. He took nine pieces of luggage and beat it in his Buick. The house peeper, whose name is Javonen—he calls himself an assistant man-

ager and security officer—is satisfied that Mitchell paid
his bill and even a week in advance for his room. He
has no worries. He doesn't like me, of course."

"Does somebody?"

"You do—five thousand dollars worth."

"Oh, you *are* an idiot. Do you think Mitchell will
come back?"

"I told you he paid a week in advance."

She sipped her drink quietly. "So you did. But that
could mean something else."

"Sure. Just spitballing, for example, I might say it
could mean that he didn't pay his bill, but someone
else did. And that the someone else wanted time to do
something—such as getting rid of that body on your
balcony last night. That is, if there was a body."

"Oh, stop it!"

She finished her drink, killed her cigarette, stood up
and left me with the check. I paid it and went back
through the lobby, for no reason that I could think of.
Perhaps by pure instinct. And I saw Goble getting into
the elevator. He seemed to have a rather strained expression. As he turned he caught my eye, or seemed to,
but he gave no sign of knowing me. The elevator went
up.

I went out to my car and drove back to the Rancho
Descansado. I lay down on the couch and went to
sleep. It had been a lot of day. Perhaps if I had a rest
and my brain cleared, I might have some faint idea of
what I was doing.

18

An hour later I was parked in front of the hardware store. It wasn't the only hardware store in Esmeralda, but it was the only one that backed on the alley called Polton's Lane. I walked east and counted the stores. There were seven of them to the corner, all shining with plate glass and chromium trim. On the corner was a dress shop with mannequins in the windows, scarves and gloves and costume jewelry laid out under the lights. No prices showing. I rounded the corner and went south. Heavy eucalyptus trees grew out of the sidewalk. They branched low down and the trunks looked hard and heavy, quite unlike the tall brittle stuff that grows around Los Angeles. At the far corner of Polton's Lane there was an automobile agency. I followed its high blank wall, looking at broken crates, piles of cartons, trash drums, dusty parking spaces, the back yard of elegance. I counted the buildings. It was easy. No questions to ask. A light burned in the small window of a tiny frame cottage that had long ago been somebody's simple home. The cottage had a wooden porch with a broken railing. It had been painted once, but that was in the remote past before the shops swallowed it up. Once it may even have had a garden. The shingles of the roof were warped. The front door was a dirty mustard yellow. The window was shut tight and

120

needed hosing off. Behind part of it hung what remained of an old roller blind. There were two steps up to the porch, but only one had a tread. Behind the cottage and halfway to the loading platform of the hardware store there was what had presumably been a privy. But I could see where a water pipe cut through the sagging side. A rich man's improvements on a rich man's property. A one-unit slum.

I stepped over the hollow place where a step would have been and knocked on the door. There was no bell push. Nobody answered. I tried the knob. Nobody had locked the door. I pushed it open and went in. I had that feeling. I was going to find something nasty inside.

A bulb burned in a frayed lamp crooked on its base, the paper shade split. There was a couch with a dirty blanket on it. There was an old cane chair, a Boston rocker, a table covered with a smeared oilcloth. On the table spread out beside a coffee cup was a copy of *El Diario,* a Spanish language newspaper, also a saucer with cigarette stubs, a dirty plate, a tiny radio which emitted music. The music stopped and a man began to rattle off a commercial in Spanish. I turned it off. The silence fell like a bag of feathers. Then the clicking of an alarm clock from beyond a half open door. Then the clank of a small chain, a fluttering sound and a cracked voice said rapidly: *"Quién es? Quién es? Quién es?"* This was followed by the angry chattering of monkeys. Then silence again.

From a big cage over in the corner the round angry eye of a parrot looked at me. He sidled along the perch as far as he could go.

"Amigo," I said.

The parrot let out a screech of insane laughter.

"Watch your language, brother," I said.

The parrot crabwalked to the other end of the perch and pecked into a white cup and shook oatmeal from his beak contemptuously. In another cup there was water. It was messy with oatmeal.

"I bet you're not even housebroken," I said.

The parrot stared at me and shuffled. He turned his

head and stared at me with his other eye. Then he leaned forward and fluttered his tail feathers and proved me right.

"Necio!" he screamed. *"Fuera!"*

Somewhere water dripped from a leaky faucet. The clock ticked. The parrot imitated the ticking amplified.

I said: "Pretty Polly."

"Hijo de la chingada," the parrot said.

I sneered at him and pushed the half-open door into what there was of a kitchen. The linoleum on the floor was worn through to the boards in front of the sink. There was a rusty three-burner gas stove, an open shelf with some dishes and the alarm clock, a riveted hot water tank on a support in the corner, the antique kind that blows up because it has no safety valve. There was a narrow rear door, closed, with a key in the lock, and a single window, locked. There was a light bulb hanging from the ceiling. The ceiling above it was cracked and stained from roof leaks. Behind me the parrot shuffled aimlessly on his perch and once in a while let out a bored croak.

On the zinc drainboard lay a short length of black rubber tubing, and beside that a glass hypodermic syringe with the plunger pushed home. In the sink were three long thin empty tubes of glass with tiny corks near them. I had seen such tubes before.

I opened the back door, stepped to the ground and walked to the converted privy. It had a sloping roof, about eight feet high in front, less than six at the back. It opened outward, being too small to open any other way. It was locked but the lock was old. It did not resist me much.

The man's scuffed toes almost touched the floor. His head was up in the darkness inches from the two by four that held up the roof. He was hanging by a black wire, probably a piece of electric light wire. The toes of his feet were pointed down as if they reached to stand on tiptoe. The worn cuffs of his khaki denim pants hung below his heels. I touched him enough to know that he was cold enough so that there was no point in cutting him down.

He had made very sure of that. He had stood by the sink in his kitchen and knotted the rubber tube around his arm, then clenched his fist to make the vein stand out, then shot a syringeful of morphine sulphate into his blood stream. Since all three of the tubes were empty, it was a fair guess that one of them had been full. He could not have taken in less than enough. Then he had laid the syringe down and released the knotted tube. It wouldn't be long, not a shot directly into the blood stream. Then he had gone out to his privy and stood on the seat and knotted the wire around his throat. By that time he would be dizzy. He could stand there and wait until his knees went slack and the weight of his body took care of the rest. He would know nothing. He would already be asleep.

I closed the door on him. I didn't go back into the house. As I went along the side towards Polton's Lane, that handsome residential street, the parrot inside the shack heard me and screeched: *"Quién es? Quién es? Quién es?"*

Who is it? Nobody, friend. Just a footfall in the night.

I walked softly, going away.

19

I WALKED softly, in no particular direction, but I knew where I would end up. I always did. At the Casa del Poniente. I climbed back into my car on Grand and circled a few blocks aimlessly, and then I was parked as usual in a slot near the bar entrance. As I got out I looked at the car beside mine. It was Goble's shabby dark little jalopy. He was as adhesive as a band-aid.

At another time I would have been racking my brains for some idea of what he was up to, but now I had a worse problem. I had to go to the police and report the hanging man. But I had no notion what to tell them. Why did I go to his house? Because, if he was telling the truth, he had seen Mitchell leave early in the morning. Why was that of significance? Because I was looking for Mitchell myself. I wanted to have a heart to heart talk with him. About what? And from there on I had no answers that would not lead to Betty Mayfield, who she was, where she came from, why she changed her name, what had happened back in Washington, or Virginia or wherever it was, that made her run away.

I had $5000 of her money in traveler's checks in my pocket, and she wasn't even formally my client. I was stuck, but good.

I walked over to the edge of the cliff and listened to

the sound of the surf. I couldn't see anything but the occasional gleam of a wave breaking out beyond the cove. In the cove the waves don't break, they slide in politely, like floorwalkers. There would be a bright moon later, but it hadn't checked in yet.

Someone was standing not far away, doing what I was doing. A woman. I waited for her to move. When she moved I would know whether I knew her. No two people move in just the same way, just as no two sets of fingerprints match exactly.

I lit a cigarette and let the lighter flare in my face, and she was beside me.

"Isn't it about time you stopped following me around?"

"You're my client. I'm trying to protect you. Maybe on my seventieth birthday someone will tell me why."

"I didn't ask you to protect me. I'm not your client. Why don't you go home—if you have a home—and stop annoying people?"

"You're my client—five thousand dollars worth. I have to do something for it—even if it's no more than growing a mustache."

"You're impossible. I gave you the money to let me alone. You're impossible. You're the most impossible man I ever met. And I've met some dillies."

"What happened to that tall exclusive apartment house in Rio? Where I was going to lounge in silk pajamas and play with your long lascivious hair, while the butler set out the Wedgwood and the Georgian silver with that faint dishonest smile and those delicate gestures, like a pansy hair stylist fluttering around a screen star?"

"Oh, shut up!"

"Wasn't a firm offer, huh? Just a passing fancy, or not even that. Just a trick to make me slaughter my sleeping hours and trot around looking for bodies that weren't there."

"Did anybody ever give you a swift poke in the nose?"

"Frequently, but sometimes I make them miss."

I grabbed hold of her. She tried to fight me off, but no fingernails. I kissed the top of her head. Suddenly she clung to me and turned her face up.

"All right. Kiss me, if it's any satisfaction to you. I suppose you would rather have this happen where there was a bed."

"I'm human."

"Don't kid yourself. You're a dirty low-down detective. Kiss me."

I kissed her. With my mouth close to hers I said: "He hanged himself tonight."

She jerked away from me violently. "Who?" she asked in a voice that could hardly speak.

"The night garage attendant here. You may never have seen him. He was on mesca, tea, marijuana. But tonight he shot himself full of morphine and hanged himself in the privy behind his shack in Polton's Lane. That's an alley behind Grand Street."

She was shaking now. She was hanging on to me as if to keep from falling down. She tried to say something, but her voice was just a croak.

"He was the guy that said he saw Mitchell leave with his nine suitcases early this morning. I wasn't sure I believed him. He told me where he lived and I went over this evening to talk to him some more. And now I have to go to the cops and tell them. And what do I tell them without telling them about Mitchell and from then on about you?"

"Please—please—*please* leave me out of it," she whispered. "I'll give you more money. I'll give you all the money you want."

"For Pete's sake. You've already given me more than I'd keep. It isn't money I want. It's some sort of understanding of what the hell I'm doing and why. You must have heard of professional ethics. Some shreds of them still stick to me. Are you my client?"

"Yes. I give up. They all give up to you in the end, don't they?"

"Far from it. I get pushed around plenty."

I got the folder of traveler's checks out of my pocket

and put a pencil flash on them and tore out five. I refolded it and handed it to her. "I've kept five hundred dollars. That makes it legal. Now tell me what it's all about."

"No. You don't have to tell anybody about that man."

"Yes, I do. I have to go to the cop house just about now. I have to. And I have no story to tell them that they won't bust open in three minutes. Here, take your goddam checks—and if you ever push them at me again, I'll smack your bare bottom."

She grabbed the folder and tore off into the darkness to the hotel. I just stood there and felt like a damn fool. I don't know how long I stood there, but finally I stuffed the five checks into my pocket and went wearily back to my car and started off to the place where I knew I had to go.

20

A MAN named Fred Pope who ran a small motel had once told me his views on Esmeralda. He was elderly, talkative, and it always pays to listen. The most unlikely people sometimes drop a fact or two that means a lot in my business.

"I been here thirty years," he said. "When I come here I had dry asthma. Now I got wet asthma. I recall when this town was so quiet dogs slept in the middle of the boulevard and you had to stop your car, if you had a car, and get out and push them out of the way. The bastards just sneered at you. Sundays it was like you was already buried. Everything shut up as tight as a bank vault. You could walk down Grand Street and have as much fun as a stiff in the morgue. You couldn't even buy a pack of cigarettes. It was so quiet you could of heard a mouse combin' his whiskers. Me and my old woman—she's been dead fifteen years now—used to play cribbage in a little place we had down on the street that goes along the cliff, and we'd listen in case something exciting would happen—like an old geezer taking a walk and tapping with a cane. I don't know if the Hellwigs wanted it that way or whether old man Hellwig done it out of spite. In them years he didn't live here. He was a big shot in the farm equipment business."

"More likely," I said, "he was smart enough to know that a place like Esmeralda would become a valuable investment in time."

"Maybe," Fred Pope said. "Anyhow, he just about created the town. And after a while he came to live here—up on the hill in one of them great big stucco houses with tile roofs. Pretty fancy. He had gardens with terraces and big green lawns and flowering shrubs, and wrought iron gates—imported from Italy, I heard, and Arizona fieldstone walks, and not just one garden, half a dozen. And enough land to keep the neighbors out of his hair. He drank a couple bottles of hooch a day and I heard he was a pretty rough customer. He had one daughter, Miss Patricia Hellwig. She was the real cream and still is.

"By that time Esmeralda had begun to fill up. At first it was a lot of old women and their husbands, and I'm tellin' you the mortician business was real good with tired old men that died and got planted by their loving widows. The goddam women last too long. Mine didn't."

He stopped and turned his head away for a moment, before he went on.

"There was a streetcar from San Diego by then, but the town was still quiet—too quiet. Not hardly anybody got born here. Child-bearing was thought kind of too sexy. But the war changed all that. Now we got guys that sweat, and tough school kids in levis and dirty shirts, and artists and country club drunks and them little gifte shoppes that sell you a two-bit highball glass for eight-fifty. We got restaurants and liquor stores, but we still don't have no billboards or poolrooms or drive-ins. Last year they tried to put in a dime-in-the-slot telescope in the park. You ought to of heard the town council scream. They killed it for sure, but the place ain't no bird refuge any more. We got as smart stores as Beverly Hills. And Miss Patricia, she spent her whole life working like a beaver to give things to the town. Hellwig died five years ago. The doctors told him he would have to cut down on the booze or he wouldn't live a year. He cussed them out and said if he couldn't take a drink when he wanted to, morning, noon or night, he'd be damned if he'd take one at all. He quit—and he was dead in a year.

"The docs had a name for it—they always have—and I guess Miss Hellwig had a name for them. Anyway, they got bumped off the staff of the hospital and that knocked them loose from Esmeralda. It didn't matter a whole lot. We still got about sixty doctors here. The town's full of Hellwigs, some with other names, but all of the family one way or another. Some are rich and some work. I guess Miss Hellwig works harder than most. She's eighty-six now, but tough as a mule. She don't chew tobacco, drink, smoke, swear or use no make-up. She give the town the hospital, a private school, a library, an art center, public tennis courts, and God knows what else. And she still gets driven in a thirty-year-old Rolls-Royce that's about as noisy as a Swiss watch. The mayor here is two jumps from a Hellwig, both downhill. I guess she built the municipal center too, and sold it to the city for a dollar. She's some woman. Of course we got Jews here now, but let me tell you something. A Jew is supposed to give you a sharp deal and steal your nose, if you ain't careful. That's all bunk. A Jew enjoys trading; he likes business, but he's only tough on the surface. Underneath a Jewish businessman is usually real nice to deal with. He's human. If you want cold-blooded skinning, we got a bunch of people in this town now that will cut you down to the bone and add a service charge. They'll take your last dollar from you between your teeth and look at you like you stole it from them."

21

THE COP HOUSE was part of a long modernistic building at the corner of Hellwig and Orcutt. I parked and
went into it, still wondering how to tell my story, and
still knowing I had to tell it.

The business office was small but very clean, and the
duty officer on the desk had two sharp creases in his
shirt, and his uniform looked as if it had been pressed
ten minutes before. A battery of six speakers on the
wall was bringing in police and sheriff's reports from
all over the county. A tilted plaque on the desk said
the duty officer's name was Griddell. He looked at me
the way they all look, waiting.

"What can we do for you, sir?" He had a cool
pleasant voice, and that look of discipline you find in
the best ones.

"I have to report a death. In a shack behind the
hardware store on Grand, in an alley called Polton's
Lane, there's a man hanging in a sort of privy. He's
dead. No chance to save him."

"Your name, please?" He was already pressing but-
tons.

"Philip Marlowe. I'm a Los Angeles private detective."

"Did you notice the number of this place?"

"It didn't have one that I could see. But it's right smack behind the Esmeralda Hardware Company."

"Ambulance call, urgent," he said into his mike. "Possible suicide in a small house behind the Esmeralda Hardware Store. Man hanging in a privy behind the house."

He looked up at me. "Do you know his name?"

I shook my head. "But he was the night garage man at the Casa del Poniente."

He flicked some sheets of a book. "We know him. Has a record for marijuana. Can't figure how he held the job, but he may be off it now, and his sort of labor is pretty scarce here."

A tall sergeant with a granite face came into the office, gave me a quick glance and went out. A car started.

The duty officer flicked a key on a small PBX. "Captain, this is Griddell on the desk. A Mr. Philip Marlowe has reported a death in Polton's Lane. Ambulance moving. Sergeant Green is on his way. I have two patrol cars in the vicinity."

He listened for a moment, then looked at me. "Captain Alessandro would like to speak to you, Mr. Marlowe. Down the hall, last door on the right, please."

He was on the mike again before I was through the swinging door.

The last door on the right had two names on it. Captain Alessandro in a plaque fastened to the wood, and Sergeant Green on a removable panel. The door was half open, so I knocked and went in.

The man at the desk was as immaculate as the desk officer. He was studying a card through a magnifying glass, and a tape recorder beside him was telling some dreary story in a crumpled, unhappy voice. The captain was about six feet three inches tall and had thick dark hair and a clear olive skin. His uniform cap was on the desk near him. He looked up, cut off the tape recorder and put down the magnifying glass and the card.

"Have a seat, Mr. Marlowe."

I sat down. He looked at me for a moment without

speaking. He had rather soft brown eyes, but his mouth was not soft.

"I understand you know Major Javonen at the Casa."

"I've met him, Captain. We are not close friends."

He smiled faintly. "That's hardly to be expected. He wouldn't enjoy private detectives asking questions in the hotel. He used to be in the CIC. We still call him Major. This is the politest goddam town I was ever in. We are a goddam smooth bunch around here, but we're police just the same. Now about this Ceferino Chang?"

"So that's his name. I didn't know."

"Yes. We know him. May I ask what you are doing in Esmeralda?"

"I was hired by a Los Angeles attorney named Clyde Umney to meet the Super Chief and follow a certain party until that party came to a stop somewhere. I wasn't told why, but Mr. Umney said he was acting for a firm of Washington attorneys and he didn't know why himself. I took the job because there is nothing illegal in following a person, if you don't interfere with that person. The party ended up in Esmeralda. I went back to Los Angeles and tried to find out what it was all about. I couldn't, so I took what I thought was a reasonable fee, two hundred and fifty, and absorbed my own expenses. Mr. Umney was not very pleased with me."

The captain nodded. "That doesn't explain why you are here or what you have to do with Ceferino Chang. And since you are not now working for Mr. Umney, unless you are working for another attorney you have no privilege."

"Give me a break, if you can, Captain. I found out that the party I was following was being blackmailed, or there was an attempt at blackmail, by a man named Larry Mitchell. He lives or lived at the Casa. I have been trying to get in touch with him, but the only information I have is from Javonen and this Ceferino Chang. Javonen said he checked out, paid his bill, and a week in advance for his room. Chang told me he left at seven A.M. this morning with nine suitcases. There was something a bit peculiar about Chang's manner, so I wanted to have another talk with him."

"How did you know where he lived?"

"He told me. He was a bitter man. He said he lived on a rich man's property, and he seemed angry that it wasn't kept up."

"Not good enough, Marlowe."

"Okay, I didn't think it was myself. He was on the weed. I pretended to be a pusher. Once in a while in my business a man has to do a good deal of faking."

"Better. But there's something missing. The name of your client—if you have one."

"Could it be in confidence?"

"Depends. We never disclose the names of blackmail victims, unless they come out in court. But if this party has committed or been indicted for a crime, or has crossed a state line to escape prosecution, then it would be my duty as an officer of the law to report her present whereabouts and the name she is using."

"Her? So you know already. Why ask me? I don't know why she ran away. She won't tell me. All I know is she is in trouble and in fear, and that somehow Mitchell knew enough to make her say uncle."

He made a smooth gesture with his hand and fished a cigarette out of a drawer. He stuck it in his mouth but didn't light it.

He gave me another steady look.

"Okay, Marlowe. For now I'll let it lay. But if you dig anything up, here is where you bring it."

I stood up. He stood up too and held his hand out.

"We're not tough. We just have a job to do. Don't get too hostile with Javonen. The guy who owns that hotel draws a lot of water around here."

"Thanks, Captain. I'll try to be a nice little boy— even to Javonen."

I went back along the hall. The same officer was on the desk. He nodded to me and I went out into the evening and got into my car. I sat with my hands tight on the steering wheel. I wasn't too used to cops who treated me as if I had a right to be alive. I was sitting there when the desk officer poked his head out of the door and called that Captain Alessandro wanted to see me again.

When I got back to Captain Alessandro's office, he was on the telephone. He nodded me to the customer's chair and went on listening and making quick notes in what looked like the sort of condensed writing that many reporters use. After a while he said: "Thanks very much. We'll be in touch."

He leaned back and tapped on his desk and frowned.

"That was a report from the sheriff's substation at Escondido. Mitchell's car has been found—apparently abandoned. I thought you might like to know."

"Thanks, Captain. Where was this?"

"About twenty miles from here, on a country road that leads to Highway 395, but is not the road a man would naturally take to get to 395. It's a place called Los Peñasquitos Canyon. Nothing there but outcrop and barren land and a dry river bed. I know the place. This morning a rancher named Gates went by there with a small truck, looking for fieldstone to build a wall. He passed a two-tone Buick hardtop parked off the side of the road. He didn't pay much attention to the Buick, except to notice that it hadn't been in a wreck, so somebody just parked it there.

"Later on in the day, around four, Gates went back to pick up another load of fieldstone. The Buick was still there. This time he stopped and looked it over. No keys in the lock, but the car wasn't locked up. No sign of any damage. Just the same, Gates wrote down the license number and the name and address on the registration certificate. When he got back to his ranch he called the substation at Escondido. Of course the deputies knew Los Peñasquitos Canyon. One of them went over and looked at the car. Clean as a whistle. The deputy managed to trick the trunk open. Empty except for a spare tire and a few tools. So he went back to Escondido and called in here. I've just been talking to him."

I lit a cigarette and offered one to Captain Alessandro. He shook his head.

"Got any ideas, Marlowe?"

"No more than you have."

"Let's hear them anyway."

"If Mitchell had some good reason to get lost and had a friend who would pick him up—a friend nobody here knew anything about—he would have stored his car in some garage. That wouldn't have made anyone curious. There wouldn't be anything to make the garage curious. They would just be storing a car. Mitchell's suitcases would already have been in his friend's car."

"So?"

"So there wasn't any friend. So Mitchell disappeared into thin air—with his nine suitcases—on a very lonely road that was hardly ever used."

"Go on from there." His voice was hard now. It had an edge to it. I stood up.

"Don't bully me, Captain Alessandro. I haven't done anything wrong. You've been very human so far. Please don't get the idea that I had anything to do with Mitchell's disappearance. I didn't—and still don't—know what he had on my client. I just know that she is a lonely and frightened and unhappy girl. When I know why, if I do manage to find out, I'll let you know or I won't. If I don't, you'll just have to throw the book at me. It wouldn't be the first time it's happened to me. I don't sell out—even to good police officers."

"Let's hope it doesn't turn out that way, Marlowe. Let's hope."

"I'm hoping with you, Captain. And thanks for treating me the way you have."

I walked back down the corridor, nodded to the duty officer on the desk and climbed back into my car again. I felt twenty years older.

I knew—and I was pretty damn sure Captain Alessandro knew too—that Mitchell wasn't alive, that he hadn't driven his car to Los Peñasquitos Canyon, but somebody had driven him there, with Mitchell lying dead on the floor of the back seat.

There was no other possible way to look at it. There are things that are facts, in a statistical sense, on paper, on a tape recorder, in evidence. And there are things that are facts because they have to be facts, because nothing makes any sense otherwise.

22

IT IS LIKE a sudden scream in the night, but there is no
sound. Almost always at night, because the dark hours
are the hours of danger. But it has happened to me
also in broad daylight—that strange, clarified moment
when I suddenly know something I have no reason for
knowing. Unless out of the long years and the long ten-
sions, and in the present case, the abrupt certainty that
what bullfighters call "the moment of truth" is here.

There was no other reason, no sensible reason at all.
But I parked across from the entrance to the Rancho
Descansado, and cut my lights and ignition, and then
drifted about fifty yards downhill and pulled the brake
back hard.

I walked up to the office. There was the small glow
of light over the night bell, but the office was closed. It
was only ten-thirty. I walked around to the back and
drifted through the trees. I came on two parked cars.
One was a Hertz rent car, as anonymous as a nickel in
a parking meter, but by bending down I could read the
license number. The car next to it was Goble's little
dark jalopy. It didn't seem very long since it was
parked by the Casa del Poniente. Now it was here.

I went on through the trees until I was below my
room. It was dark, soundless. I went up the few steps
very slowly and put my ear to the door. For a little

while I heard nothing. Then I heard a strangled sob—a man's sob, not a woman's. Then a thin, low cackling laugh. Then what seemed to be a hard blow. Then silence.

I went back down the steps and through the trees to my car. I unlocked the trunk and got out a tire iron. I went back to my room as carefully as before—even more carefully. I listened again. Silence. Nothing. The quiet of the night. I reached out my pocket flash and flicked it once at the window, then slid away from the door. For several minutes nothing happened. Then the door opened a crack.

I hit it hard with my shoulder and smashed it wide open. The man stumbled back and then laughed. I saw the glint of his gun in the faint light. I smashed his wrist with the tire iron. He screamed. I smashed his other wrist. I heard the gun hit the floor.

I reached back and switched the lights on. I kicked the door shut.

He was a pale-faced redhead with dead eyes. His face was twisted with pain, but his eyes were still dead. Hurt as he was, he was still tough.

"You ain't going to live long, boy," he said.

"You're not going to live at all. Get out of my way."

He managed to laugh.

"You've still got legs," I said. "Bend them at the knees and lie down—face down—that is, if you want a face."

He tried to spit at me, but his throat choked. He slid down to his knees, holding his arms out. He was groaning now. Suddenly he crumpled. They're so goddam tough when they hold the stacked deck. And they never know any other kind of deck.

Goble was lying on the bed. His face was a mass of bruises and cuts. His nose was broken. He was unconscious and breathing as if half strangled.

The redhead was still out, and his gun lay on the floor near him. I wrestled his belt off and strapped his ankles together. Then I turned him over and went through his pockets. He had a wallet with $670 in it, a driver's license in the name of Richard Harvest, and the address of a small hotel in San Diego. His pocketbook contained numbered checks on about twenty banks, a set of credit cards, but no gun permit.

I left him lying there and went down to the office. I pushed the button of the night bell, and kept on pushing it. After a while a figure came down through the dark. It was Jack in a bathrobe and pajamas. I still had the tire iron in my hand.

He looked startled. "Something the matter, Mr. Marlowe?"

"Oh, no. Just a hoodlum in my room waiting to kill me. Just another man beaten to pieces on my bed. Nothing the matter at all. Quite normal around here, perhaps."

"I'll call the police."

"That would be awfully damn nice of you, Jack. As you see, I am still alive. You know what you ought to do with this place? Turn it into a pet hospital."

He unlocked the door and went into the office. When I heard him talking to the police I went back to my room. The redhead had guts. He had managed to get into a sitting position against the wall. His eyes were still dead and his mouth was twisted into a grin.

I went over to the bed. Goble's eyes were open.

"I didn't make it," he whispered. "Wasn't as good as I thought I was. Got out of my league."

"The cops are on their way. How did it happen?"

"I walked into it. No complaints. This guy's a life-taker. I'm lucky. I'm still breathing. Made me drive over here. He cooled me, tied me up, then he was gone for a while."

"Somebody must have picked him up, Goble. There's a rent car beside yours. If he had that over at the Casa, how did he get back there for it?"

Goble turned his head slowly and looked at me. "I thought I was a smart cookie. I learned different. All I want is back to Kansas City. The little guys can't beat the big guys—not ever. I guess you saved my life."

Then the police were there.

First two prowl car boys, nice cool-looking serious men in the always immaculate uniforms and the always deadpan faces. Then a big tough sergeant who said his name was Sergeant Holzminder, and that he was the cruising sergeant on the shift. He looked at the redhead and went over to the bed.

"Call the hospital," he said briefly, over his shoulder.

One of the cops went out to the car. The sergeant bent down over Goble. "Want to tell me?"

"The redhead beat me up. He took my money. Stuck a gun into me at the Casa. Made me drive him here. Then he beat me up."

"Why?"

Goble made a sighing sound and his head went lax on the pillow. Either he passed out again or faked it. The sergeant straightened up and turned to me. "What's your story?"

"I haven't any, Sergeant. The man on the bed had dinner with me tonight. We'd met a couple of times. He said he was a Kansas City PI. I never knew what he was doing here."

"And this?" The sergeant made a loose motion towards the redhead, who was still grinning a sort of unnatural epileptic grin.

"I never saw him before. I don't know anything about him, except that he was waiting for me with a gun."

"That your tire iron?"

"Yes, Sergeant."

The other cop came back into the room and nodded to the sergeant. "On the way."

"So you had a tire iron," the sergeant said coldly. "So why?"

"Let's say I just had a hunch someone was waiting for me here."

"Let's try it that you didn't have a hunch, that you already knew. And knew a lot more."

"Let's try it that you don't call me a liar until you know what you're talking about. And let's try it that you don't get so goddam tough just because you have three stripes. And let's try something more. This guy may be a hood, but he still has two broken wrists, and you know what that means, Sergeant? He'll never be able to handle a gun again."

"So we book you for mayhem."

"If you say so, Sergeant."

Then the ambulance came. They carried Goble out first and then the intern put temporary splints on the two wrists of the redhead. They unstrapped his ankles. He looked at me and laughed.

"Next time, pal, I'll think of something original—but you did all right. You really did."

He went out. The ambulance doors clanged shut and the growling sound of it died. The sergeant was sitting down now, with his cap off. He was wiping his forehead.

"Let's try again," he said evenly. "From the beginning. Like as if we didn't hate each other and were just trying to understand. Could we?"

"Yes, Sergeant. We could. Thanks for giving me the chance."

23

EVENTUALLY I landed back at the cop house. Captain Alessandro had gone. I had to sign a statement for Sergeant Holzminder.

"A tire iron, huh?" he said musingly. "Mister, you took an awful chance. He could have shot you four times while you were swinging on him."

"I don't think so, Sergeant. I bumped him pretty hard with the door. And I didn't take a full swing. Also, maybe he wasn't supposed to shoot me. I don't figure he was in business for himself."

A little more of that, and they let me go. It was too late to do anything but go to bed, too late to talk to anyone. Just the same I went to the telephone company office and shut myself in one of the two neat outdoor booths and dialed the Casa del Poniente.

"Miss Mayfield, please. Miss Betty Mayfield. Room 1224."

"I can't ring a guest at this hour."

"Why? You got a broken wrist?" I was a real tough boy tonight. "Do you think I'd call if it wasn't an emergency?"

He rang and she answered in a sleepy voice.

"This is Marlowe. Bad trouble. Do I come there or do you come to my place?"

"What? What kind of trouble?"

"Just take it from me for just this once. Should I pick you up in the parking lot?"

"I'll get dressed. Give me a little time."

I went out to my car and drove to the Casa. I was smoking my third cigarette and wishing I had a drink when she came quickly and noiselessly up to the car and got in.

"I don't know what this is all about," she began, but I interrupted her.

"You're the only one that does. And tonight you're going to tell me. And don't bother getting indignant. It won't work again."

I jerked the car into motion and drove fast through silent streets and then down the hill and into the Rancho Descansado and parked under the trees. She got out without a word and I unlocked my door and put the lights on.

"Drink?"

"All right."

"Are you doped?"

"Not tonight, if you mean sleeping pills. I was out with Clark and drank quite a lot of champagne. That always makes me sleepy."

I made a couple of drinks and gave her one. I sat down and leaned my head back.

"Excuse me," I said. "I'm a little tired. Once in every two or three days I have to sit down. It's a weakness I've tried to get over, but I'm not as young as I was. Mitchell's dead."

Her breath caught in her throat and her hand shook. She may have turned pale. I couldn't tell.

"Dead?" she whispered. "Dead?"

"Oh, come off it. As Lincoln said, you can fool all of the detectives some of the time, and some of the detectives all the time, but you can't—"

"Shut up! Shut up right now! Who the hell do you think you are?"

"Just a guy who has tried very hard to get where he could do you some good. A guy with enough experience and enough understanding to know that you were in some kind of jam. And wanted to help you out of it, with no help from you."

"Mitchell's dead," she said in a low breathless voice. "I didn't mean to be nasty. Where?"

"His car has been found abandoned in a place you wouldn't know. It's about twenty miles inland, on a road that's hardly used. A place called Los Peñasquitos Canyon. A place of dead land. Nothing in his car, no suitcases. Just an empty car parked at the side of a road hardly anybody ever uses."

She looked down at her drink and took a big gulp. "You said he was dead."

"It seems like weeks, but it's only hours ago that you came over here and offered me the top half of Rio to get rid of his body."

"But there wasn't—I mean, I must just have dreamed—"

"Lady, you came over here at three o'clock in the morning in a state of near-shock. You described just where he was and how he was lying on the chaise on your little porch. So I went back with you and climbed the fire stairs, using the infinite caution for which my profession is famous. And no Mitchell, and then you asleep in your little bed with your little sleeping pill cuddled up to you."

"Get on with your act," she snapped at me. "I know how you love it. Why didn't *you* cuddle up to me? I wouldn't have needed a sleeping pill—perhaps?"

"One thing at a time, if you don't mind. And the first thing is that you were telling the truth when you came here. Mitchell *was* dead on your porch. But someone got his body out of there while you were over here making a sucker out of me. And somebody got him down to his car and then packed his suitcases and got them down. All this took time. It took more than time. It took a great big reason. Now who would do a thing like that—just to save you the mild embarrassment of reporting a dead man on your porch?"

"Oh, shut up!" She finished her drink and put the

glass aside. "I'm tired. Do you mind if I lie down on your bed?"

"Not if you take your clothes off."

"All right—I'll take my clothes off. That's what you've been working up to, isn't it?"

"You might not like that bed. Goble was beaten up on it tonight—by a hired gun named Richard Harvest. He was really brutalized. You remember Goble, don't you? The fat sort of man in the little dark car that followed us up the hill the other night."

"I don't know anybody named Goble. And I don't know anybody named Richard Harvest. How do you know all this? Why were they here—in your room?"

"The hired gun was waiting for me. After I heard about Mitchell's car I had a hunch. Even generals and other important people have hunches. Why not me? The trick is to know when to act on one. I was lucky tonight—or last night. I acted on a hunch. He had a gun, but I had a tire iron."

"What a big strong unbeatable man you are," she said bitterly. "I don't mind the bed. Do I take my clothes off now?"

I went over and jerked her to her feet and shook her. "Stop your nonsense, Betty. When I want your beautiful white body, it won't be while you're my client. I want to know what you are afraid of. How the hell can I do anything about it if I don't know? Only you can tell me."

She began to sob in my arms.

Women have so few defenses, but they certainly perform wonders with those they have.

I held her tight against me. "You can cry and cry and sob and sob, Betty. Go ahead, I'm patient. If I wasn't that—well, hell, if I wasn't that—"

That was as far as I got. She was pressed tight to me trembling. She lifted her face and dragged my head down until I was kissing her.

"Is there some other woman?" she asked softly, between my teeth.

"There have been."

"But someone very special?"

"There was once, for a brief moment. But that's a long time ago now."

"Take me. I'm yours—all of me is yours. Take me."

24

A BANGING on the door woke me. I opened my eyes
stupidly. She was clinging to me so tightly that I could
hardly move. I moved her arms gently until I was free.
She was still sound asleep.

I got out of bed and pulled a bathrobe on and went
to the door; I didn't open it.

"What's the matter? I was asleep."

"Captain Alessandro wants you at the office right
away. Open the door."

"Sorry, can't be done. I have to shave and shower
and so on."

"Open the door. This is Sergeant Green."

"I'm sorry, Sergeant. I just can't. But I'll be along
just as soon as I can make it."

"You got a dame in there?"

"Sergeant, questions like that are out of line. I'll be
there."

I heard his steps go down off the porch. I heard
someone laugh. I heard a voice say, "This guy is really
rich. I wonder what he does on his day off."

I heard the police car going away. I went into the
bathroom and showered and shaved and dressed. Betty
was still glued to the pillow. I scribbled a note and put
in on my pillow. "The cops want me. I have to go.
You know where my car is. Here are the keys."

I went out softly and locked the door and found the Hertz car. I knew the keys would be in it. Operators like Richard Harvest don't bother about keys. They carry sets of them for all sorts of cars.

Captain Alessandro looked exactly as he had the day before. He would always look like that. There was a man with him, an elderly stony-faced man with nasty eyes.

Captain Alessandro nodded me to the usual chair. A cop in uniform came in and put a cup of coffee in front of me. He gave me a sly grin as he went out.

"This is Mr. Henry Cumberland of Westfield, Carolina, Marlowe. North Carolina. I don't know how he found his way out here, but he did. He says Betty Mayfield murdered his son."

I didn't say anything. There was nothing for me to say. I sipped the coffee which was too hot, but good otherwise.

"Like to fill us in a little, Mr. Cumberland?"

"Who's this?" He had a voice as sharp as his face.

"A private detective named Philip Marlowe. He operates out of Los Angeles. He is here because Betty Mayfield is his client. It seems that you have rather more drastic ideas about Miss Mayfield than he has."

"I don't have any ideas about her, Captain," I said. "I just like to squeeze her once in a while. It soothes me."

"You like being soothed by a murderess?" Cumberland barked at me.

"Well, I didn't know she was a murderess, Mr. Cumberland. It's all news to me. Would you care to explain?"

"The girl who calls herself Betty Mayfield—and that was her maiden name—was the wife of my son, Lee Cumberland. I never approved of the marriage. It was one of those wartime idiocies. My son received a broken neck in the war and had to wear a brace to protect his spinal column. One night she got it away from him and taunted him until he rushed at her. Unfortunately, he had been drinking rather heavily since he came home, and there had been quarrels. He tripped and fell across the bed. I came into the room and found her trying to put the brace back on his neck. He was already dead."

I looked at Captain Alessandro. "Is this being recorded, Captain?"

He nodded. "Every word."

"All right, Mr. Cumberland. There's more, I take it."

"Naturally. I have a great deal of influence in Westfield. I own the bank, the leading newspaper, most of the industry. The people of Westfield are my friends. My daughter-in-law was arrested and tried for murder and the jury brought in a verdict of guilty."

"The jury were all Westfield people, Mr. Cumberland?"

"They were. Why shouldn't they be?"

"I don't know, sir. But it sounds like a one-man town."

"Don't get impudent with me, young man."

"Sorry, sir. Would you finish?"

"We have a peculiar law in our state, and I believe in a few other jurisdictions. Ordinarily the defense attorney makes an automatic motion for a directed verdict of not guilty and it is just as automatically denied. In my state the judge may reserve his ruling until after the verdict. The judge was senile. He reserved his ruling. When the jury brought in a verdict of guilty, he declared in a long speech that the jury had failed to consider the possibility that my son had in a drunken rage removed the brace from his neck in order to terrify his wife. He said that where there was so much bitterness anything was possible, and that the jury had failed to consider the possibility that my daughter-in-law might have been doing exactly what she said she was doing—trying to put the brace back on my son's neck. He voided the verdict and discharged the defendant.

"I told her that she had murdered my son and that I

would see to it that she had no place of refuge anywhere on this earth. That is why I am here."

I looked at the captain. He looked at nothing. I said: "Mr. Cumberland, whatever your private convictions, Mrs. Lee Cumberland, whom I know as Betty Mayfield, has been tried and acquitted. You have called her a murderess. That's a slander. We'll settle for a million dollars."

He laughed almost grotesquely. "You small-town nobody," he almost screamed. "Where I come from you would be thrown into jail as a vagrant."

"Make it a million and a quarter," I said. "I'm not so valuable as your ex-daughter-in-law."

Cumberland turned on Captain Alessandro. "What goes on here?" he barked. "Are you all a bunch of crooks?"

"You're talking to a police officer, Mr. Cumberland."

"I don't give a good goddam what you are," Cumberland said furiously. "There are plenty of crooked police."

"It's a good idea to be sure—before you call them crooked," Alessandro said, almost with amusement. Then he lit a cigarette and blew smoke and smiled through it.

"Take it easy, Mr. Cumberland. You're a cardiac case. Prognosis unfavorable. Excitement is very bad for you. I studied medicine once. But somehow I became a cop. The war cut me off, I guess."

Cumberland stood up. Spittle showed on his chin. He made a strangled sound in his throat. "You haven't heard the last of this," he snarled.

Alessandro nodded. "One of the interesting things about police work is that you never hear the last of anything. There are always too many loose ends. Just what would you like me to do? Arrest someone who has been tried and acquitted, just because you are a big shot in Westfield, Carolina?"

"I told her I'd never give her any peace," Cumberland said furiously. "I'd follow her to the end of the earth. I'd make sure everyone knew just what she was!"

"And what is she, Mr. Cumberland?"

"A murderess that killed my son and was let off by an idiot of a judge—that's what she is!"

Captain Alessandro stood up, all six feet three inches of him. "Take off, buster," he said coldly. "You annoy me. I've met all kinds of punks in my time. Most of them have been poor stupid backward kids. This is the first time I've come across a great big important man who was just as stupid and vicious as a fifteen-year-old delinquent. Maybe you own Westfield, North Carolina, or think you do. You don't own a cigar butt in my town. Get out before I put the arm on you for interfering with an officer in the performance of his duties."

Cumberland almost staggered to the door and groped for the knob, although the door was wide open. Alessandro looked after him. He sat down slowly.

"You were pretty rough, Captain."

"It's breaking my heart. If anything I said makes him take another look at himself—oh well, hell!"

"Not his kind. Am I free to go?"

"Yes. Goble won't make charges. He'll be on his way back to Kansas City today. We'll dig up something on this Richard Harvest, but what's the use? We put him away for a while, and a hundred just like him are available for the same work."

"What do I do about Betty Mayfield?"

"I have a vague idea that you've already done it," he said, deadpan.

"Not until I know what happened to Mitchell." I was just as deadpan as he was.

"All I know is that he's gone. That doesn't make him police business."

I stood up. We gave each other those looks. I went out.

25

SHE WAS still asleep. My coming in didn't wake her. She slept like a little girl, soundlessly, her face at peace. I watched her for a moment, then lit a cigarette and went out to the kitchen. When I had put coffee on to percolate in the handsome paper-thin dime store aluminum percolator provided by the management, I went back and sat on the bed. The note I had left was still on the pillow with my car keys.

I shook her gently and her eyes opened and blinked.

"What time is it?" she asked, stretching her bare arms as far as she could. "God, I slept like a log."

"It's time for you to get dressed. I have some coffee brewing. I've been down to the police station—by request. Your father-in-law is in town, Mrs. Cumberland."

She shot upright and stared at me without breathing.

"He got the brush, but good, from Captain Alessandro. He can't hurt you. Was that what all the fear was about?"

"Did he say—say what happened back in Westfield?"

"That's what he came here to say. He's mad enough to jump down his own throat. And what of it? You didn't, did you? Do what they said?"

"I did not." Her eyes blazed at me.

153

"Wouldn't matter if you had—now. But it wouldn't make me very happy about last night. How did Mitchell get wise?"

"He just happened to be there or somewhere nearby. Good heavens, the papers were full of it for weeks. It wasn't hard for him to recognize me. Didn't they have it in the papers here?"

"They ought to have covered it, if only because of the unusual legal angle. If they did, I missed it. The coffee ought to be ready now. How do you take it?"

"Black, please. No sugar."

"Fine. I don't have any cream or sugar. Why did you call yourself Eleanor King? No, don't answer that. I'm stupid. Old man Cumberland would know your unmarried name."

I went out to the kitchen and removed the top of the percolator, and poured us both a cup. I carried hers to her. I sat down in a chair with mine. Our eyes met and were strangers again.

She put her cup aside. "That was good. Would you mind looking the other way while I gather myself together?"

"Sure." I picked a paperback off the table and made a pretense of reading it. It was about some private eye whose idea of a hot scene was a dead naked woman hanging from the shower rail with the marks of torture on her. By that time Betty was in the bathroom. I threw the paperback into the wastebasket, not having a garbage can handy at the moment. Then I got to thinking there are two kinds of women you can make love to. Those who give themselves so completely and with such utter abandonment that they don't even think about their bodies. And there are those who are self-conscious and always want to cover up a little. I remembered a girl in a story by Anatole France who insisted on taking her stockings off. Keeping them on made her feel like a whore. She was right.

When Betty came out of the bathroom she looked like a fresh-opened rose, her make-up perfect, her eyes shining, every hair exactly in place.

"Will you take me back to the hotel? I want to speak to Clark."

"You in love with him?"

"I thought I was in love with you."

"It was a cry in the night," I said. "Let's not try to make it more than it was. There's more coffee out in the kitchen."

"No, thanks. Not until breakfast. Haven't you ever been in love? I mean enough to want to be with a woman every day, every month, every year?"

"Let's go."

"How can such a hard man be so gentle?" she asked wonderingly.

"If I wasn't hard, I wouldn't be alive. If I couldn't ever be gentle, I wouldn't deserve to be alive."

I held her coat for her and we went out to my car. On the way back to the hotel she didn't speak at all. When we got there and I slid into the now familiar parking slot, I took the five folded traveler's checks out of my pocket and held them out to her.

"Let's hope it's the last time we pass these back and forth," I said. "They're wearing out."

She looked at them, but didn't take them. "I thought they were your fee," she said rather sharply.

"Don't argue, Betty. You know very well that I couldn't take money from you."

"After last night?"

"After nothing. I just couldn't take it. That's all. I haven't done anything for you. What are you going to do? Where are you going? You're safe now."

"I've no idea. I'll think of something."

"Are you in love with Brandon?"

"I might be."

"He's an ex-racketeer. He hired a gunman to scare Goble off. The gunman was ready to kill me. Could you really love a man like that?"

"A woman loves a man. Not what he is. And he may not have meant it."

"Goodbye, Betty. I gave it what I had, but it wasn't enough."

She reached her hand out slowly and took the checks. "I think you're crazy. I think you're the craziest man I ever met." She got out of the car and walked away quickly, as she always did.

26

I GAVE HER time to clear the lobby and go up to her room, and then I went into the lobby myself and asked for Mr. Clark Brandon on a house phone. Javonen came by and gave me a hard look, but he didn't say anything.

A man's voice answered. It was his all right.

"Mr. Brandon, you don't know me, although we shared an elevator the other morning. My name is Philip Marlowe. I'm a private detective from Los Angeles, and I'm a friend of Miss Mayfield. I'd like to talk to you a little, if you'll give me the time."

"I seem to have heard something about you, Marlowe. But I'm all set to go out. How about a drink around six this evening?"

"I'd like to get back to Los Angeles, Mr. Brandon. I won't keep you long."

"All right," he said grudgingly. "Come on up."

He opened the door, a big, tall, very muscular man in top condition, neither hard nor soft. He didn't offer to shake hands. He stood aside, and I went in.

"You alone here, Mr. Brandon?"

"Sure. Why?"

"I wouldn't want anyone else to hear what I have to say."

"Well say it and get done."

He sat in a chair and put his feet up on an ottoman. He flicked a gold lighter at a gold-tipped cigarette. Big deal.

"I first came down here on the instructions of a Los Angeles lawyer to follow Miss Mayfield and find out where she went, and then report back. I didn't know why and the lawyer said he didn't either, but that he was acting for a reputable firm of attorneys in Washington. Washington, D.C."

"So you followed her. So what?"

"So she made contact with Larry Mitchell, or he with her, and he had a hook of some sort into her."

"Into a lot of women from time to time," Brandon said coldly. "He specialized in it."

"He doesn't any more, does he?"

He stared at me with cool blank eyes. "What's that mean?"

"He doesn't do anything any more. He doesn't exist any more."

"I heard he left the hotel and went off in his car. What's it to do with me?"

"You didn't ask me how I know he doesn't exist any more."

"Look, Marlowe." He flicked ash from his cigarette with a contemptuous gesture. "It could be that I don't give a damn. Get to what concerns me, or get out."

"I also got involved down here, if involved is the word, with a man named Goble who said he was a private eye from Kansas City, and had a card which may or may not have proved it. Goble annoyed me a good deal. He kept following me around. He kept talking about Mitchell. I couldn't figure what he was after. Then one day at the desk you got an anonymous letter. I watched you read it over and over. You asked the clerk who left it. The clerk didn't know. You even picked the empty envelope out of the wastebasket. And when you went up in the elevator you didn't look happy."

Brandon was beginning to look a little less relaxed. His voice had a sharper edge.

"You could get too nosy, Mr. PI. Ever think of that?"

"That's a silly question. How else would I make a living?"

"Better get out of here while you can still walk."

I laughed at him, and that really burned him. He shot to his feet and came striding over to where I was sitting.

"Listen, boy friend. I'm a pretty big man in this town. I don't get pushed around much by small-time operators like you. Out!"

"You don't want to hear the rest?"

"I said, out!"

I stood up. "Sorry. I was prepared to settle this with you privately. And don't get the idea that I'm trying to put a bite on you—like Goble. I just don't do those things. But if you toss me out—without hearing me out—I'll have to go to Captain Alessandro. He'll listen."

He stood glowering for a long moment. Then a curious sort of grin appeared on his face.

"So he'll listen to you. So what? I could get him transferred with one phone call."

"Oh, no. Not Captain Alessandro. He's not brittle. He got tough with Henry Cumberland this morning. And Henry Cumberland isn't a man that's used to having anyone get tough with him, any place, any time. He just about broke Cumberland in half with a few contemptuous words. You think you could get that guy to lay off? You should live so long."

"Jesus," he said, still grinning, "I used to know guys like you once. I've lived here so long now I must have forgotten they still make them. Okay. I'll listen."

He went back to the chair and picked another gold-tipped cigarette from a case and lit it. "Care for one?"

"No thanks. This boy Richard Harvest—I think he was a mistake. Not good enough for the job."

"Not nearly good enough, Marlowe. Not nearly. Just a cheap sadist. That's what comes of getting out of touch. You lose your judgment. He could have scared

Goble silly without laying a finger on him. And then taking him over to your place—what a laugh! What an amateur! And look at him now. No good for anything any more. He'll be selling pencils. Would you care for a drink?"

"I'm not on that kind of terms with you, Brandon. Let me finish. In the middle of the night—the night I made contact with Betty Mayfield, and the night you chased Mitchell out of The Glass Room—and did it very nicely, I might add—Betty came over to my room at the Rancho Descansado. One of your properties, I believe. She said Mitchell was dead on a chaise on her porch. She offered me large things to do something about it. I came back over here and there was no man dead on her porch. The next morning the night garage man told me Mitchell had left in his car with nine suitcases. He'd paid his bill and a week in advance to hold his room. The same day his car was found abandoned in Los Peñasquitos Canyon. No suitcases, no Mitchell."

Brandon stared hard at me, but said nothing.

"Why was Betty Mayfield afraid to tell me what she was afraid of? Because she had been convicted of murder in Westfield, North Carolina, and then the verdict was reversed by the judge, who has that power in that state, and used it. But Henry Cumberland, the father of the husband she was accused of murdering, told her he would follow her anywhere she went and see that she had no peace. Now she finds a dead man on her porch. And the cops investigate and her whole story comes out. She's frightened and confused. She thinks she couldn't be lucky twice. After all, a jury did convict her."

Brandon said softly: "His neck was broken. He fell over the end wall of my terrace. She couldn't have broken his neck. Come out here. I'll show you."

We went out on the wide sunny terrace. Brandon marched to the end wall and I looked down over it and I was looking straight down on a chaise on Betty Mayfield's porch.

"This wall isn't very high," I said. "Not high enough to be safe."

"I agree," Brandon said calmly. "Now suppose he was standing like this"—he stood with his back against the wall, and the top of it didn't come very much above the middle of his thighs. And Mitchell had been a tall man too—"and he goads Betty into coming over near enough so that he can grab her, and she pushes him off hard, and over he goes. And he just happens to fall in such a way—by pure chance—that his neck snaps. And that's exactly how her husband died. Do you blame the girl for getting in a panic?"

"I'm not sure I blame anybody, Brandon. Not even you."

He stepped away from the wall and looked out to sea and was silent for a moment. Then he turned.

"For nothing," I said, "except that you managed to get rid of Mitchell's body."

"Now, how in hell could I do that?"

"You're a fisherman, among other things. I'll bet that right here in this apartment you have a long strong cord. You're a powerful man. You could get down to Betty's porch, you could put that cord under Mitchell's arms, and you have the strength to lower him to the ground behind the shrubbery. Then, already having his key out of his pocket, you could go to his room and pack up all his stuff, and carry it down to the garage, either in the elevator, or down the fire stairs. That would take three trips. Not too much for you. Then you could drive his car out of the garage. You probably knew the night man was a doper and that he wouldn't talk, if he knew you knew. This was in the small hours of the night. Of course the garage man lied about the time. Then you could drive the car as near as possible to where Mitchell's body was, and dump him into it, and drive off to Los Peñasquitos Canyon."

Brandon laughed bitterly. "So I am in Los Peñasquitos Canyon with a car and a dead man and nine suitcases. How do I get out of there?"

"Helicopter."

"Who's going to fly it?"

"You. They don't check much on helicopters yet, but they soon will, because they are getting more and more numerous. You could have one brought to you in Los Peñasquitos Canyon, having arranged in advance, and you could have had someone come along to pick up the pilot. A man in your position can do almost anything, Brandon."

"And then what?"

"You loaded Mitchell's body and his suitcases into the helicopter and flew out to sea and set the helicopter hovering close to the water, and then you could dump the body and the suitcases, and drift on back to wherever the helicopter came from. A nice clean well-organized job."

Brandon laughed raucously—too raucously. The laugh had a forced sound.

"You think I'd actually be idiot enough to do all this for a girl I had only just met?"

"Uh-uh. Think again, Brandon. You did it for you. You forget Goble. Goble came from Kansas City. Didn't *you*?"

"What if I did?"

"Nothing. End of the line. But Goble didn't come out here for the ride. And he wasn't looking for Mitchell, unless he already knew him, and between them, they figured they had a gold mine. You were the gold mine. But Mitchell got dead and Goble tried to go it alone, and he was a mouse fighting with a tiger. But would you want to explain how Mitchell fell off your terrace? Would you want an investigation of your background? What so obvious as for the police to think you had thrown Mitchell over the wall? And even if they couldn't prove it, where would you be in Esmeralda from then on?"

He walked slowly to the far end of the terrace and back. He stood in front of me, his expression completely blank.

"I could have you killed, Marlowe. But in some strange way in the years I have lived here, I don't seem to be that kind of guy any more. So you have me licked. I don't have any defense, except to have you killed. Mitchell was the lowest kind of man, a blackmailer of women. You could be right all along the line, but I wouldn't regret it. And it's just possible, believe me, just possible that I too went out on a limb for Betty Mayfield. I don't expect you to believe it, but it *is* possible. Now, let's deal. How much?"

"How much for what?"

"For not going to the cops."

"I already told you how much. Nothing. I just wanted to know what happened. Was I approximately right?"

"Dead right, Marlowe. Right on the nose. They may get me for it yet."

"Maybe. Well, I'll take myself out of your hair now. Like I said—I want to get back to Los Angeles. Somebody might offer me a cheap job. I have to live, or do I?"

"Would you shake hands with me?"

"No. You hired a gun. That puts you out of the class of people I shake hands with. I might be dead today, if I hadn't had a hunch."

"I didn't mean him to kill anyone."

"You hired him. Goodbye."

27

I GOT OUT of the elevator and Javonen seemed to be waiting for me. "Come into the bar," he said. "I want to talk to you."

We went into the bar, which was very quiet at that hour. We sat at a corner table. Javonen said quietly: "You think I'm a bastard, don't you?"

"No. You have a job. I have a job. Mine annoyed you. You didn't trust me. That doesn't make you a bastard."

"I try to protect the hotel. Who do you try to protect?"

"I never know. Often, when I do know, I don't know how. I just fumble around and make a nuisance of myself. Often I'm pretty inadequate."

"So I heard—from Captain Alessandro. If it's not too personal, how much do you make on a job like this?"

"Well, this was a little out of the usual line, Major. As a matter of fact, I didn't make anything."

"The hotel will pay you five thousand dollars—for protecting its interests."

"The hotel, meaning Mr. Clark Brandon."

"I suppose. He's the boss."

"It has a sweet sound—five thousand dollars. A very

sweet sound. I'll listen to it on my way back to Los Angeles." I stood up.

"Where do I send the check, Marlowe?"

"The Police Relief Fund could be glad to have it. Cops don't make much money. When they get in trouble they have to borrow from the Fund. Yes, I think the Police Relief Fund would be very grateful to you."

"But not you?"

"You were a major in the CIC. You must have had a lot of chances to graft. But you're still working. I guess I'll be on my way."

"Listen, Marlowe. You're being a damn fool. I want to tell you—"

"Tell yourself, Javonen. You have a captive audience. And good luck."

I walked out of the bar and got into my car. I drove to the Descansado and picked up my stuff and stopped at the office to pay my bill. Jack and Lucille were in their usual positions. Lucille smiled at me.

Jack said: "No bill, Mr. Marlowe. I've been instructed. And we offer you our apologies for last night. But they're not worth much, are they?"

"How much would the bill be?"

"Not much. Twelve-fifty maybe."

I put the money on the counter. Jack looked at it and frowned. "I said there was no bill, Mr. Marlowe."

"Why not? I occupied the room."

"Mr. Brandon—"

"Some people never learn, do they? Nice to have known you both. I'd like a receipt for this. It's deductible."

28

I DIDN'T DO more than ninety back to Los Angeles. Well, perhaps I hit a hundred for a few seconds now and then. Back on Yucca Avenue I stuck the Olds in the garage and poked at the mailbox. Nothing, as usual. I climbed the long flight of redwood steps and unlocked my door. Everything was the same. The room was stuffy and dull and impersonal as it always was. I opened a couple of windows and mixed a drink in the kitchen. I sat down on the couch and stared at the wall. Wherever I went, whatever I did, this was what I would come back to. A blank wall in a meaningless room in a meaningless house.

I put the drink down on a side table without touching it. Alcohol was no cure for this. Nothing was any cure but the hard inner heart that asked for nothing from anyone.

The telephone started to ring. I picked it up and said emptily: "Marlowe speaking."

"Is this Mr. Philip Marlowe?"

"Yes."

"Paris has been trying to reach you, Mr. Marlowe. I'll call you back in a little while."

I put the phone down slowly and I think my hand shook a little. Driving too fast, or not enough sleep.

The call came through in fifteen minutes: "The

party calling you from Paris is on the line, sir. If you have any difficulty, please flash your operator."

"This is Linda. Linda Loring. You remember me, don't you, darling?"

"How could I forget?"

"How are you?"

"Tired—as usual. Just came off a very trying sort of case. How are you?"

"Lonely. Lonely for you. I've tried to forget you. I haven't been able to. We made beautiful love together."

"That was a year and a half ago. And for one night. What am I supposed to say?"

"I've been faithful to you. I don't know why. The world is full of men. But I've been faithful to you."

"I haven't been faithful to you, Linda. I didn't think I'd ever see you again. I didn't know you expected me to be faithful."

"I didn't. I don't. I'm just trying to say that I love you. I'm asking you to marry me. You said it wouldn't last six months. But why not give it a chance? Who knows—it might last forever. I'm begging you. What does a woman have to do to get the man she wants?"

"I don't know. I don't even know how she knows she wants him. We live in different worlds. You're a rich woman, used to being pampered. I'm a tired hack with a doubtful future. Your father would probably see to it that I didn't even have that."

"You're not afraid of my father. You're not afraid of anyone. You're just afraid of marriage. My father knows a man when he sees one. Please, please, please. I'm at the Ritz. I'll send you a plane ticket at once."

I laughed. "You'll send *me* a plane ticket? What sort of guy do you think I am? I'll send *you* a plane ticket. And that will give you time to change your mind."

"But, darling, I don't need you to send me a plane ticket. I have—"

"Sure. You have the money for five hundred plane tickets. But this one will be *my* plane ticket. Take it, or don't come."

"I'll come, darling. I'll come. Hold me in your arms.

Hold me close in your arms. I don't want to own you. Nobody ever will. I just want to love you."

"I'll be here. I always am."

"Hold me in your arms."

The phone clicked, there was a buzzing sound, and then the line went dead.

I reached for my drink. I looked around the empty room—which was no longer empty. There was a voice in it, and a tall slim lovely woman. There was a dark hair on the pillow in the bedroom. There was that soft gentle perfume of a woman who presses herself tight against you, whose lips are soft and yielding, whose eyes are half blind.

The telephone rang again. I said: "Yes?"

"This is Clyde Umney, the lawyer. I don't seem to have had any sort of satisfactory report from you. I'm not paying you to amuse yourself. I want an accurate and complete account of your activities at once. I demand to know in full detail exactly what you have been doing since you returned to Esmeralda."

"Having a little quiet fun—at my own expense."

His voice rose to a sharp cackle. "I demand a full report from you at once. Otherwise I'll see that you get bounced off your license."

"I have a suggestion for you, Mr. Umney. Why don't you go kiss a duck?"

There were sounds of strangled fury as I hung up on him. Almost immediately the telephone started to ring again.

I hardly heard it. The air was full of music.